JEDI QUEST

JEDI QUEST

BY JUDE WATSON

PATH TO TRUTH

SCHOLASTIC INC.

New York   Toronto   London   Auckland   Sydney
Mexico City   New Delhi   Hong Kong   Buenos Aires

ISBN 0-439-24204-5

12 11 10 9 8 7 6 5 4 3 2 1   1 2 3 4 5 6/0

Printed in the U.S.A.
First Scholastic printing, September 2001

JEDI QUEST

No one on Tatooine could remember a day this fine. The two suns shone, but their rays did not blister the skin. The wind blew, but it was a gentle wind that did not bring choking dust and sand. The normally brutal climate had loosened its grip. Most of the moisture farmers, smugglers, and slaves of Tatooine didn't have the time or energy to look up from their hard lives to notice it.

Seven-year-old Anakin Skywalker did. When his mother, Shmi, opened the windows at dawn, the two of them stood breathing in the fresh air with wonder. For the first time in a long while, Anakin considered himself lucky. Today the weather was good, and he had his first afternoon off.

Day after day he was cooped up in Watto's junk shop. He was a slave, but it wasn't the worst job he could imagine. He learned about hyperspace engines and power converters and droid motivators. He could assemble a reactivate switch blindfolded. The only trouble was, he had to work for the Toydarian Watto, whose temper and greed constantly surprised Anakin, growing worse by the day.

Anakin crammed his breakfast in his mouth as he hurried through the crowded streets of Mos Espa toward Watto's shop. He broke into a run, sliding easily between two careening eopies. Today Watto had to make a journey to Anchorhead. He had heard of a spectacular crash between two sand skimmers and a space frigate, and he was anxious to be first to bid for the parts.

The trip placed Watto in a bind, for his excitement at the thought of striking a deal battled with his irritation at closing the store for a day. All week the air had been full of the angry buzzing of Watto's wings and his muttered comments about how life was unfair to hardworking beings like him.

Watto couldn't bear to lose money, even for a day, but he didn't trust Anakin to run the shop. Neither could he bear to give his slave a day off. So Watto had left Anakin a long list of chores to do, a list long enough to guarantee that Anakin would be in the closed shop from sunrise to sundown.

What Watto didn't count on was that Anakin had friends to help him. Not living beings — everyone he knew his age was a slave, too. Anakin considered droids his friends, and he knew that with their help he could get his chores done in half the time.

As soon as he reached the shop, he programmed the droids and got to work. Many of the droids were old models or half fixed, but he managed to keep them going. By midday, the chores were done.

Anakin picked up the pack Shmi had filled with meat pies and fruit that morning. He hurried all the way back to where he lived, breathing deep lungfuls of air as he ran. His friend Amee was a house slave for a rich Toong couple. They gave her one afternoon off a month. This was it.

Amee waited outside on the steps of her dwelling in the crowded, layered stack of hovels in Mos Espa. Her chestnut hair was worn in a braided crown around her head. She had woven some yellow flowers through her braids. It added to the holiday feeling of this day. Her thin face, usually so serious, looked almost pretty as she smiled.

"I've never been on a picnic," she said. "Mother says she used to go on them when she was a girl."

Amee's mother, Hala, opened the door and smiled

at Anakin. Her job was to work on transmitter parts at home. "I'm glad you'll both get to enjoy the day. Don't go far."

"I know just the spot," Anakin told her.

Amee followed him through the crowded lanes and streets of Mos Espa. There were even more beings packed in the streets today. Amee and Anakin had learned how to move through the streets almost invisibly, avoiding the fierce tempers of the spacers and smugglers.

Anakin knew exactly where they should share their picnic, even though he'd never been on one, either. He had found the spot weeks before while searching for junked parts on the outskirts of the space-port.

Tatooine's hills were sandy and barren, but nestled among them Anakin had discovered a small canyon. There, he found a tree with flickering green-gold leaves. He had never seen the species before, and it was the first time he had seen such a color in a natural form. Tatooine was a land of variations of beige and tan.

The tree was scrawny and struggled to survive, but when you sat underneath it and closed your eyes, you could hear the rustle of dry leaves. On a day like today, with the air so fresh, you could almost pretend you were on a beautiful green planet.

"It's perfect," Amee breathed.

They feasted on Shmi's meat pies and Hala's turnovers. They drank sweet juice and planned their futures, which always included Anakin liberating all the slaves on Tatooine. The sun slid lower in the sky. Suddenly, the afternoon was over.

"I guess we'd better get back," Anakin said reluctantly.

"I hate being a slave," Amee said. She shoved the food wrappings into her pack with unusual force.

There wasn't any reply Anakin could make. They *all* hated being slaves. Anakin vowed that someday Shmi would live a soft, pleasant life, filled with leisure and good things to eat, just like this day. He would see to it.

He and Amee slogged through the sandy hills and down into the streets of Mos Espa. To their surprise, the streets were now almost empty, the food stalls shuttered.

"What's going on?" Anakin wondered. "It's like there's a sandstorm coming, but the air is so clear."

As they got closer to their homes, their unease increased. On the outskirts, they saw shattered entrances and wreckage in the street. They passed a man crying into his hands. Sobs shook his thin shoulders.

Anakin and Amee exchanged a wordless glance. The fear that always hummed under the surface of their lives sparked and became a living current. Something was very wrong.

A woman ran by them, her eyes streaming tears. "Elza!" she screamed. "Elza!"

"Elza Monimi," Amee said, panic beginning to shade her voice. "He's our neighbor. What's happening?"

They began to run. Every other house seemed to be damaged. Beings mingled in the streets, asking one another for news of daughters, sons, mothers, whole families. They heard a whispered name, a name repeated over and over in tones of dread and horror.

Anakin stopped a neighbor, Titi Chronelle. "What happened?"

"Slave raid," Titi told him. "Pirates. Led by Krayn. With blasters and restraining devices. They have transmitters that override our own. They can steal whoever they want. Many were taken." Titi spoke in short bursts, as if he could not manage a whole sentence.

Anakin felt his own breath leave him. "My mother?"

Titi looked at him sadly before rushing on. "I don't know."

Without another word, Amee took off toward her own dwelling. Anakin ran, his heart bursting, his legs pumping. He charged into his home. He looked around wildly.

Everything seemed the same. But where was Shmi?

Then he saw her in the corner. Her knees were drawn up against her chest, her head buried. As he started toward her, she jerked her head up.

For a moment, he saw sheer terror in her face. Shock paralyzed him. He had never seen his mother afraid. For him, she was the image of calm strength. She held all the terrors of life at bay for him.

As she took in his expression, the wild look in her eyes instantly disappeared. The warm light he knew so well came back. She held out her arms to him, and he rushed to her.

"I didn't know where you were," she said.

He felt her strong arms surround him and buried his face in the familiar scent of her clothes. She rocked him gently.

"You're shaking," she said. "Hush, Annie. We're both safe."

Somehow he knew that the terror he'd seen on her face was not just because she could not find him. It was because of what she had seen. Of what had almost happened to her.

But that fear, the fear that his mother could disappear, that she could be hurt or killed, that she could be at the mercy of her own terror, was just too great for him to face. He pushed the thought of her anguished face away and breathed in her warmth, felt the strength and gentleness of her hands soothing him. Instantly, the shaking stopped. He told himself he had not seen her vulnerability. His mother could not be vanquished. She could not be taken. She could not be hurt. The core of her was strength. She could keep them both safe. That was his reality. Somehow Anakin knew that if he acknowledged Shmi's fear he would close the door on his own childhood. He wasn't ready to do that. He was seven years old. He needed her too much.

Outside, they heard voices. A deep voice calling, trying to override a high, frightened one.

"Amee! Come back!"

"Where's my mother?"

Anakin looked up. "It's Amee."

Shmi's grip on him tightened. "Hala was taken by the slave raiders."

He looked into her face. The terror was gone, but

sadness was there now, deep sadness and compassion, and also something else, something remote that he could not decipher. As though she knew something he did not, and would not tell him — he did not want or need to know.

"It is a terrible thing to be a slave on Tatooine, Annie," Shmi whispered. "But it could be far, far worse for us."

She pushed his hair off his forehead. The remote look left her eyes. "But you are safe," she said in a firm voice. "We are together. Now, come. Let us do what we can to comfort Amee and her father."

Anakin rose. He stood on the threshold of his dwelling for a moment, watching Shmi cross to console Amee and her father. Owners were now walking among the milling beings, checking on the slaves. Anakin saw Hala's owner, Yor Millto. Millto was checking off something on a datapad.

"A nuisance, to lose Hala," he said to his assistant. "This will cost me. But she wasn't highly skilled. Easy to replace."

Anakin's gaze went to Amee. Her face was buried in Shmi's robes, and her thin shoulders shook with her wracking sobs. Hala's husband sat nearby, his face in his hands.

Easy to replace . . .

Pain tore through Anakin, pain he did not want to face.

He made a vow. He knew he had an extraordinary memory. Organization and learning came easily to him. He would use that power to sear this memory into his mind and heart. When he needed this, he would recall every detail — the exact shade of blue of the sky, the heartbreaking quality of Amee's uncontrollable sobs.

There was only one thing he would train his mind not to recall, one thing he never wanted to see again, even in memory — the terror he had glimpsed on his mother's face.

Obi-Wan Kenobi squinted through the viewscreen of the small, sleek craft, a transport on loan from the Senate. Mist swirled around and below him. He could not see a landing site.

"Anything?" Anakin asked. With zero visibility, his Padawan was using instruments to pilot the transport. That, and his sure connection to the Force. At only thirteen years of age, Anakin was already an expert pilot, even better than Obi-Wan. Obi-Wan would be the first to admit it.

"Not yet. The mist will clear in a moment." He hoped. He knew that the craggy peaks of the ice mountains were close. The trick was to find a landing site.

"And then will you tell me why we're here?" Anakin asked.

"All in good time." Obi-Wan noted that the mist was

beginning to thin. Patches of a lighter gray streaked through the clouds. Suddenly, as the craft lowered, the icy peaks appeared, looming out of the clouds, a flash of silver against a sea of gray.

Obi-Wan consulted the coordinates for his destination, then searched the crags for a likely landing spot. All he could see around him was the blinding white of ice and snow. He knew that the seemingly sheer mountainsides concealed ledges and hidden caves. Sheets of ice made for treacherous possibilities.

At last he spotted a ledge that was protected from the wind. It was clear of snow and he saw only isolated patches of ice. It would be a tight fit, and there was always the danger the craft would slide on the ice straight off the ledge, but he knew his Padawan could do it.

"There," he told Anakin, and gave the coordinates.

The boy looked at him, surprised. "Really?"

"You can do it."

"I know I can do it," Anakin said. "I'm just wondering why you *want* me to."

"Because it's an easy climb to our destination from there."

Anakin flipped switches to begin the landing procedures. "And I know better than to ask what that is."

Obi-Wan sat back and watched in admiration as,

with cool nerves and a steady hand, Anakin expertly maneuvered the ship into the tight space. He set the ship down as gently as if their landing pad were a nest of kroyie eggs. There would be just enough room to activate the hatch and clamber out.

Anakin looked out the viewscreen at the sheer icy cliffs surrounding them. "Can you tell me what this planet is, at least?"

"Ilum," Obi-Wan answered, watching his Padawan's expression carefully.

The name brought a spark of recognition to Anakin's face. His bright eyes flashed. Still, he kept his tone guarded. "I see."

"We are not here on a mission," Obi-Wan continued. "It is a quest. It is here that you will gather the crystals to fashion your own lightsaber."

Anakin's sober face cracked with the grin that Obi-Wan had come to look forward to seeing, a smile that radiated pleasure and hope.

"Thank you for this honor," he said.

"You are ready," Obi-Wan replied.

"The Council thinks so?" Anakin asked.

It was a shrewd question. As a matter of fact, the Council was divided on Anakin Skywalker's readiness to take on the full rights of a Jedi. There were those who thought he had come to Jedi training too late.

They worried about the anger and fear that he pushed away deep inside him. They worried about his early life as a slave, about his fierce ties to the mother who had let him go.

Yoda and Mace Windu were among those who were cautious, and who had given Obi-Wan many uneasy moments. He respected their viewpoint too much to discount it completely.

But his promise to his former Master, Qui-Gon Jinn, was more important. Qui-Gon had been dead for four years now, but he was such a vivid presence in Obi-Wan's life that he considered their bond just as strong. Taking on Anakin as his Padawan was not only a vow to his beloved former Master, but also the right thing to do.

In the end, Obi-Wan had to trust his own instincts. Yoda and Mace Windu must trust them, too. He had lobbied hard in order to bring his Padawan here, and finally, the Council could not oppose him.

He hoped his decision was the right one. In his short time at the Temple, Anakin's progress had been astonishing. By everything that was measurable, he exceeded expectations. He was at the top of his class in lightsaber training, piloting, memory skills, and the most important goal of all — connection to the Force.

Yet it was exactly his quick progress that gave

Obi-Wan pause. Things came too easily to him. There was a danger of recklessness and arrogance inherent in his power. Anakin had a tendency to take matters into his own hands. He could be impetuous and make his own way, disregarding advice.

Just as Obi-Wan once did. Just as Qui-Gon once did. That was what Obi-Wan always came back to. He had made grave mistakes at Anakin's age. He wanted to allow Anakin the freedom to do the same.

They pulled on their winter survival gear, fastening thermal coats over their tunics and pulling gloves over their hands. They lowered goggles over their eyes. The temperatures on Ilum were numbingly cold. Blizzards struck without warning. Ice formations had treacherous sharp edges.

They opened the hatch and carefully stepped onto the icy ground. There was only a small amount of ledge between them and a drop of thousands of meters. The wind cut into the exposed parts of their bodies, the tips of their noses and chins. The sun was just a pale suggestion in the sky, a frosty color almost indistinguishable from the white sky and the colors of ice and snow.

"Where is the Crystal Cave?" Anakin asked.

Obi-Wan pointed. "Up. We have to scale this cliff."

Anakin regarded the cliff carefully. It was a sheer

sheet of blue ice, smooth as a mirror. There were no handholds or footholds visible. Any misstep would send them flying into the open air.

"So this is the easy climb," he said. "Tell me something. Why did the Jedi choose such a hazardous spot to keep the Ilum crystals? Wouldn't it make sense to remove them from the cavern and keep them in a safe place? Even a thousand years ago, they had to have a better idea."

"The crystals grow in the cave," Obi-Wan answered as he reached for the cable launcher on his utility belt. "This is where we must gather them. The challenge is part of the reward."

The wind whipped a strand of stray sandy hair away from Anakin's cheek. His gaze snapped with the exhilaration of the adventure ahead. "I'm not complaining. It looks like fun." He flashed a mischievous grin.

Obi-Wan nodded. There was something about this boy that wound around his heart. During the course of their missions together he had seen firsthand Anakin's impulsive generosity, his loyalty, his thirst to learn.

Remember, Padawan, that most beings are essentially unknowable. There are mysteries at the heart that can surprise even those who think they know themselves.

Obi-Wan turned away so that Anakin could not see his wry smile. Qui-Gon was in his head so often. It was as though his presence was so powerful that he could never die. Obi-Wan was grateful for it. He missed his friend and Master with a keenness that had not diminished with the years.

He activated the cable launcher and the sharp spike bit into the ice above. He tested the line.

"Remember to factor in the wind," he told Anakin. "There is wind shear on the mountain. The gusts can come from any direction. Keep your body loose. Pay attention to balance at all times. The ice is not as smooth as it appears. There will be formations that can cut you."

Anakin nodded. The dancing light had left his eyes; they now seemed opaque and expressionless. Obi-Wan recognized the look. Anakin had an ability to summon stillness in a moment. He went somewhere that Obi-Wan could not reach. Obi-Wan knew he was gathering his will and the Force for the difficult climb ahead.

Anakin launched his own cable and tested it. After a nod from Obi-Wan, the two activated the lines and let themselves be hauled up at dizzying speed to hang suspended. Obi-Wan chipped at the ice with a sharp implement to create his next foothold. He glanced over to make sure that Anakin was doing the same.

Suddenly the biting wind gusted. It hit him broadside, causing him to momentarily sway against the ice cliff. Obi-Wan twisted so that his shoulder protected his face from the ice.

He slipped one foot into the crevice he'd created and hauled himself up slightly. Then he created a crevice for one hand. This was the tricky part, requiring perfect balance. Carefully, he loosened his cable launcher for the next assault on the ice. The wind suddenly flipped around from the other direction, slamming him against the ice. He lay as flat as he could against the cliff, digging in with his fingers. It felt as though a giant hand was trying to fling him off the face of the mountain.

As soon as the wind gusts subsided, he activated the cable line again. Only two more launches and they would be at the high, narrow ledge that opened out into the Crystal Cave.

Anakin had already launched himself high in the air. He worked quickly with his sharp tool, digging another foothold into the ice cliff. Obi-Wan could see that despite his speed Anakin was struggling with the wind gusts that slammed him against the cliff.

Obi-Wan took the lead in order to slow Anakin's

pace a bit. They leapfrogged up the cliff, pausing to wait out the wind gusts. At last Obi-Wan was able to reach the lip of the cliff above. He looked over at Anakin, who gave him a nod. At the same moment, they launched themselves up to the safety of the cliff ledge.

But they were not safe. Obi-Wan paused, teetering a bit on the edge. Surprise caused him to almost step back. A group of gorgodons were lying directly in front of them, sleeping near the mouth of the Crystal Cave. They were large, hulking creatures native to Ilum. Usually their feeding grounds were on the icy plains below, where they thrived on lichen and scrub. Obi-Wan knew that they were expert climbers, but he had never heard of them up this high.

They were also fierce predators. "Be still," he whispered to Anakin. If they were lucky, the beasts would not see them. Their eyesight was poor, but their hearing and sense of smell were excellent.

"What are they?" Anakin breathed.

"Gorgodons," Obi-Wan murmured. "Triple rows of teeth, sharp claws. They dispatch their victims by squeezing them to death. The only way to kill them is a blow to the back of the neck."

Anakin regarded them warily. "Anything else?" he whispered as a gust of wind swept the ledge.

The wind must have carried their scent, for one of the gigantic creatures stirred. "Yes," Obi-Wan said. "Watch out for their —"

Suddenly a large, reptilian tail whipped out from the closest gorgodon, smacking Anakin and sending him flying back toward the cliff edge.

"Tails!" Obi-Wan shouted, vaulting after him.

CHAPTER 2

Anakin was thrown back by the force of the blow. His foot slid on an ice patch, sending him careening close to the edge of the cliff.

Obi-Wan leaped. With one arm, he kept his light-saber slashing at the tail, which continued to flail toward Anakin. With the other hand, he reached out and yanked Anakin to safety.

Anakin recovered his balance immediately and activated his training lightsaber. It was not capable of the same power as a Jedi lightsaber, but it could protect him somewhat. It was up to Obi-Wan to ensure that his Padawan wasn't vulnerable.

The gorgodons were roused now. They awoke in a fury, jaws snapping and eyes rolling. They roared, the fur sticking up now in sharp spikes. They bared their triple rows of sharp yellow teeth at the intruders.

Obi-Wan and Anakin had no choice. The gorgodons were prepared to fight to the death.

As usual before a battle, Obi-Wan's mind went clear and still.

Look for the weakness in the strength.

Yes, Qui-Gon, Obi-Wan thought. *Their great size makes them powerful, but it also makes them clumsy. I will use that.*

The largest gorgodon loped toward him. It had the dead relentless gaze of a predator as it raised a paw as big as a gravsled to swat Obi-Wan. He was sure he would be sent flying off the cliff if it connected.

The blow was slow in coming, at least for the reflexes of a Jedi. Obi-Wan had time to contemplate his move and the likely counterattack. Mindful of Anakin, he rolled to the right, drawing the gorgodon in that direction. The creature swung out with its tail as it missed, as Obi-Wan expected it to. Obi-Wan struck a blow to the gorgodon's side. He felt the impact shudder through his lightsaber. The skeletal structure of the gorgodon was extraordinarily strong, as well as covered by deep layers of fat and muscle. It would take more than one blow to fell such a creature.

At the same time, Anakin leaped to the side, slashing at the giant paw with his lightsaber. The creature gave a howl as the two blows connected. It whirled around with surprising speed, the lethal tail whipping forward toward Anakin. This time the boy was prepared. He leaped backward, somersaulting in the air to give himself momentum. When he came down, he delivered a blow to the gorgodon's nose that surprised the animal.

Another roar brought the other gorgodons closer to protect their comrade. Tails slashed and paws rose, claws ripping at their clothing. There was little time for Obi-Wan or Anakin to strike any effective blows. They were too busy trying to stay out of the way.

Suddenly Obi-Wan's foot hit a patch of black ice. Hidden by the shadows, the ice was slick and deadly. He slid helplessly straight toward the gorgodon. The great beast bared its yellow teeth and raised its massive arms to pin him between them.

Anakin accessed the Force and leaped as high as he could. He came down on a paw, which flicked him off like a flimsy durasheet. The boy flew back and hit the cave wall, dazed.

Obi-Wan regained his balance and struck out in a furious series of moves. His lightsaber was a blur as he dived, feinted, and reversed, striking blow after blow at the gorgodon's paws and body. The blows wouldn't kill it, but they did slow it down. One angry, earsplitting roar followed another. Obi-Wan moved so fast the gorgodon could not track him.

Anakin's head cleared and he raced forward to join Obi-Wan. He did not notice that another gorgodon had craftily moved to cut him off. Anakin was directly in the creature's path, caught between the gorgodon and the sheer cliff.

Obi-Wan leaped forward. The only course open to him was to place himself between the creature and Anakin. He struck out at the creature's face with his lightsaber, but he saw the giant paws come together, trapping him. Obi-Wan's breath left his body at the blow. The gorgodon brought Obi-Wan to his chest in a death-hug.

Obi-Wan's face was buried in the foul-smelling fur. He choked, struggling to fill his lungs. Instead, he breathed fur. The animal squeezed him tighter. He was afraid his ribs would crack. His last reserves of breath whooshed out of his body. He tried to move his arms, but he was pinned.

Out of the corner of his eye, he saw a blur. A second later the animal howled, and its grip loosened just a bit. He realized that Anakin had used his cable launcher. The sharp end had dug into the gorgodon's fleshy back. Now Anakin was above him, on top of the creature.

The gorgodon's grip intensified. Obi-Wan fought to stay conscious as his vision went gray. He kicked out with his feet, but it was like kicking the face of the mountain.

Just when he thought he could hold out no longer, the gorgodon's grip lessened and its arms opened, dropping Obi-Wan abruptly to the hard ground. He scrambled out of the way as the animal fell dead. Clinging to the gorgodon's neck, Anakin launched himself off the animal's body to land clear. He'd been able to fell the creature at the soft, vulnerable point in its neck.

The other gorgodons smelled the death of their comrade. With surprising speed, they dug their sharp claws into the cliff face and began to scramble up the ice to the next peak.

Panting, Anakin turned off his training lightsaber. Obi-Wan rose slowly to his feet, still struggling to catch his breath. They both paused, their clothing torn by the gorgodon's claws, their hair matted with sweat. Obi-Wan peeled off his goggles and Anakin did the same.

He grinned at his Padawan. "Thanks for that. Now comes the hard part."

Anakin wiped sweat off his forehead. "Glad to hear it. I was getting bored."

Despite his words, Obi-Wan could see that the battle had drained Anakin. His Padawan hated to show weakness. Yet Obi-Wan also knew that Anakin would recover quickly.

"We should remove our survival gear here," Obi-Wan said, stripping off his gloves. "We won't need it inside the cave. The crystals are deep within. To reach them, you will have to pass through visions and voices. Some of them may frighten you. Some of them are drawn from your own past. They are your deepest fears. That is what you must face."

Anakin now stood in his tunic. The cold wind did not cause him to shiver. His shoulders squared, and he took a step toward the cave. "I am ready."

Obi-Wan put a hand on his sleeve. "Remember your training, Anakin," he said. "Let your fear enter you. Do not battle it. There is no shame in it. Your feelings are your strength. Experience them and let them go as you proceed toward your goal. There are lessons to be learned even from fear and anger. Face those lessons and move on with calm and justice."

"I know all these things," Anakin said, a trace of impatience in his voice.

"No," Obi-Wan said softly, "you do not. But you will."

Once inside the cave, they were plunged into darkness. The walls of the cave were of black stone. The stone was smooth and shiny, but it swallowed light rather than reflected it. Entering the cave was like entering a void.

"Should I use a glow rod?" Anakin's voice echoed.

"No. Wait for your eyes to adjust."

Obi-Wan reached into his tunic and took out a small pouch. He placed it in Anakin's hand. "Here is the hilt you worked on and the other components. After you find the crystals, you will fashion the lightsaber to your own hand. Do not rush the task. Some Jedi take days or weeks to make it. However long it takes you, I will wait. We will stay on Ilum as long as necessary."

Now they could distinguish the shape of the walls around them and the stray rocks in their path. Obi-Wan walked farther into the cave and gestured at the black walls. "Here is our history."

Over the centuries, Jedi history had been recorded on the walls of the cave. The drawings were made of strong shapes and lines, just enough to suggest the truth of a scene or the character of a Jedi. Names were inscribed in rows that went from the ceiling to the floor. There were also signs and symbols that Obi-Wan and Anakin didn't understand.

Go back. Here is what you fear.

The voice was a murmur, more like a running brook. Anakin looked at Obi-Wan questioningly.

"It begins now," Obi-Wan said softly. "You must go forward alone."

A Jedi stepped forward from the cave wall. His tunic fell all the way to the tips of his bare feet. The lightsaber he held looked like an ancient weapon. His expression was so fierce that Anakin stopped dead. "There are so many pleasures in the galaxy. Why do you deprive yourself? The Jedi path is narrow. Why choose it? It will only bring you grief."

Obi-Wan waited to see what his Padawan would do. The time for his instruction was over. After a moment, Anakin walked forward, and the Jedi Knight disappeared.

Anakin was soon swallowed up by the darkness of the cave. Obi-Wan could wait by the entrance, but he had only been to the cave once, years ago, and he found his curiosity just as strong. His steps took him farther into the cave. He was willing to lose sight of Anakin; he knew his Padawan must face the cave alone. But he did not want him to get too far away.

He saw a shape move toward him. A tall Jedi, powerfully built but still graceful. A rugged face with compassionate eyes.

"Master," he breathed.

Qui-Gon smiled.

Obi-Wan's heart cracked. Joy rushed through him. Tears sprang to his eyes.

"I have missed you."

Qui-Gon said nothing. He made a gesture across his throat, as though he could not speak. His image, Obi-Wan saw now, shimmered faintly.

Suddenly, Qui-Gon whirled and his lightsaber was in his hand. He struck again and again at an unseen enemy. Obi-Wan stumbled back, his hand on the hilt of his lightsaber. He knew that this was not truly Qui-Gon, that his Master was not in danger, but the impulse to help was so strong he nearly drew his weapon.

Before he could do so, Qui-Gon suddenly staggered. Now he was facing Obi-Wan. He saw the shock in his Master's eyes.

It was how he had looked when he'd received the death blow from the Sith Lord.

"No!" Obi-Wan shouted. He could not relive that moment again. He could not. *This is not my test, Master. It is my Padawan's. Do not do this to me. . . .*

Qui-Gon fell to his knees. His eyes remained on Obi-Wan. The sadness in his gaze tore into Obi-Wan, searing and hot.

The image disappeared, only to reappear a heartbeat later. Again, he saw Qui-Gon double over. Again, he saw him sink to his knees. Obi-Wan was as helpless to reach out as he'd been four years earlier. Was he being taunted with his own failure to prevent his Master's death?

"No," Obi-Wan whispered.

Again and again, he was forced to relive Qui-Gon's slow dying. He groped for calm but could not find it. All he could feel was pain. He raged again at his helplessness. Trapped behind the energy bars, he had watched his Master fall. It was the central event of his life. Why was he forced to relive it here?

On his knees, Qui-Gon reached out to Obi-Wan. This time, the image did not fade. Grief choked Obi-Wan as he took a half step toward his Master.

Something was different this time. Qui-Gon's eyes were not filmed with pain. They were clear. They were holding a message. A warning. A plea. Obi-Wan did not know.

"What is it, Master? What are you telling me?"

Qui-Gon shook his head helplessly. His hand trembled as he reached out to Obi-Wan. His fingers could almost touch Obi-Wan's tunic. As they came closer, the image dissolved into shimmering sparks of light.

Obi-Wan was so shaken he fell to his knees as Qui-Gon had. He felt the dampness of his cheeks, marked by tears. He had been given a message, but he could not decipher it.

All he knew was that he had just faced his greatest fear. Since Qui-Gon's death, he had been afraid that he would let down Qui-Gon even as he struggled to uphold his legacy. Was Qui-Gon warning him that he was in danger of failing, after all?

CHAPTER 3

Visions and voices. Shadows and echoes. What was so hard about this?

Anakin strode confidently into the depths of the cave. Jedi appeared and disappeared. Voices murmured at him to retreat, that he did not want to face what he had come to face. That despite his connection to the Force, he would never be a true Jedi.

Anakin shook off the voices. He knew the differences between things he could fight and things he could not. Why be afraid of shadows?

Then he stopped dead. He saw himself.

He was seven or eight years old and wore the rough garments of a slave. He sat in a corner by the cave wall, tinkering with an unseen object. Anakin heard the sound of a bell. A musical sound, light and pleasing.

Suddenly, the bell rolled directly toward him. He

flinched and it stopped at his feet. Blood poured from the opening and spilled over his boots.

It isn't blood, he told himself. He could hear his racing heart pound in his ears. *Shadows and echoes. That's all it is.*

He was relieved when the vision of himself disappeared. A moment later a woman emerged from the darkness, her hair down around her shoulders. Shmi.

"Mother. Mom —"

She did not hear him or see him. She ran straight past him. Tendrils of hair stuck to her cheeks. Her face was shiny with sweat. The sweat of terror. He smelled her terror, felt the air move his hair.

He turned, but she disappeared. Then when he turned forward, there she was. She ran toward him again, her face stretched by horror.

This he could not bear. Anakin squeezed his eyes shut. When he opened them again, another figure had joined Shmi. A huge man, more like a creature than a human. Anakin could not see his face, which was in shadow. He grabbed Shmi roughly and threw her to the ground like a pile of rubbish.

"No!" Anger pounded in him, and he rushed forward. He seemed to hit an invisible wall and bounced back. The shadowy figure raised a hand to Shmi. She curled up in a ball to absorb the blow. Her knees were drawn up and her head was tucked down. There was something familiar about the posture that caused dread to fill Anakin.

"No!" Anakin shouted.

Shmi looked directly at him for the first time. He saw the fear, the terror. This seemed familiar to him as well, as though it were a memory rather than a vision. But had he ever seen his mother afraid? Not that he could remember.

He wanted to bury himself in her arms, feel her strength, but he could not. He could not make the fear on her face go away. Was he seeing something that had actually happened? Or was he seeing the future? At that thought, his own fear rose.

Anakin felt the fear as a living thing, an oozing organism that filled his body and threatened to choke him. He fought against it. Fear would make him soft. He would make the fear hard. He would twist it and make it into a weapon. A weapon of anger. Anger was productive.

Obi-Wan had told him to accept the fear. He could not do it. If he breathed it in, it would fill his lungs and choke him. But anger he could direct.

"I'll kill you!" he shouted to the shadowy figure.

The shadowy figure laughed.

"I will!" Anakin ran at the shadow and could not reach him. The vision disintegrated into particles of light.

With a last despairing look, Shmi disappeared as well.

In frustration, Anakin slammed his hand against the cave wall. Blood began to ooze from fissures.

You cannot save her, a voice said. *No matter how many times you tell yourself you will. It is a dream. She lives the nightmare.*

"Stop," he begged. "Stop."

As if the cave itself had heard him, everything stopped. The cave wall was smooth again. What had looked like blood was now just moisture. The darkness fell around him like a heavy blanket.

Shakily, Anakin moved forward. He felt sweat trickle down his forehead and cheeks. Ahead he saw a faint gleam on the floor of the cave.

"The crystals," a voice said.

He turned. It was Obi-Wan. His Master smiled at him. "It's time."

Anakin's step quickened. He leaned down to examine the cave floor. The crystals grew in intricate formations. Even in the dark cave, they glowed. He passed his hand over them without touching. He felt vibrations emanate from them. Slowly, he chose the three that seemed to speak to him. To his surprise, it was easy to break the pieces free. He placed them in the pouch hanging from his utility belt.

"Before you begin, you must meditate," Obi-Wan said. "Go into a trance state, Anakin. Cleanse your mind. Then your feelings will guide your intent."

Anakin sat on the floor of the cave. He emptied the contents of the pouch onto his lap. He held the three crystals in his palm. They had a strange warmth.

Accessing the Force was not difficult for him, even now. He felt it rise around him from the dirt and rocks and air, and especially from the crystals themselves. He felt comforted by that sureness.

"Now begin." Obi-Wan's voice was soft.

His Master gave him a gentle, encouraging smile. But suddenly, Obi-Wan's face changed. Strange markings covered his skin. Horns sprouted from his bald head. The smile became a smirk, and Anakin saw blackness and evil.

It was Qui-Gon's murderer. Obi-Wan had described him in detail.

Anakin sprang to his feet, scattering the crystals.

"Did I startle you?" the Sith Lord asked. He began to circle around Anakin. "Perhaps you need to work on those Jedi reflexes. You're almost as clumsy as Qui-Gon."

Rage pumped through Anakin. Qui-Gon had risked so much to take Anakin away. He had been the one to see that Anakin could be a Jedi Knight. Anakin owed him everything. He reached for his training lightsaber, but it flew out of his hand.

The Sith laughed. "A child's toy. Try this." He threw something at Anakin. It was a fully fashioned lightsaber, beautifully balanced, with an austere hilt. Just the kind of lightsaber Anakin would make.

He activated it, and the laser glowed red.

"Why do you fear your anger?" the Sith Lord asked. In a casual gesture, he activated his own double-edged lightsaber. "Why do you fear your hate? I can feel it. You hate me. It is natural." He bared his teeth. "After all, I gutted your friend like an animal."

With a howl torn from his belly, Anakin threw himself at the Sith. Their lightsabers tangled. Their faces were close. He could smell the Sith's foul metallic breath.

"You see?" Anakin's enemy purred. "You see what anger can do? It gives you power. It is something you can use, like a weapon. You thought the same thing a moment ago. You will twist your fear into a weapon. Why deny it?"

"No," Anakin said, driving his lightsaber toward the Sith again. "I will learn to let my anger go. I am a Jedi."

"Fool," Qui-Gon's killer hissed. "There are other paths to power."

"It isn't power I seek," Anakin said, his lightsaber tangling with the Sith's again. The shock of the blow made him grip his lightsaber with both hands.

"Then you lie," the dark Lord said, stepping back. "How else will you save that poor, weeping mother you abandoned if you do not have power?"

Anger surged again. Anakin whirled, his lightsaber circling, his body taut. The blow passed through his enemy.

The Sith laughed. "Don't you remember, boy? I am just a vision. Your vision. I am the Master you secretly want. I am the one who will deliver to you what you most desire."

"No!" Anakin screamed. He launched himself forward. Again and again he tried to strike a blow, using every technique he had mastered. The Sith's own lightsaber whirled in a circle, deflecting Anakin's moves.

With a cunning twist, the Sith flipped Anakin's lightsaber from his grasp. It spun in the air, then disintegrated into pieces. Then he reached out a hand. Anakin felt the Force move against his body. He flew through the air and hit the cave wall. His head hit the hard stone and he slid down. When his head cleared, he found himself sitting on the floor, the pieces of the lightsaber in his lap.

"The dark side can deliver what you most desire," the Sith Lord said, leaning over him. Anakin could feel his hot breath on his cheek. How could a vision have breath?

"Admit it," Qui-Gon's killer said. He raised his lightsaber for the killing blow.

Anakin summoned up the last shreds of his defiance. He stared down his foe. "I have created you. I can make you go."

His arms still over his head, his lightsaber pulsing, the Sith smiled. "But I will return. I dwell inside you."

He disappeared, and there was only blackness. Anakin looked down. A completed lightsaber lay in his lap, the very lightsaber the Sith had tossed to him. Was it real? He picked it up and turned it in his hand. He gripped it, and it seemed solid against his fingers, a perfect fit. He activated it, and the shaft of the laser glowed blue, surprising him.

Anakin stood, locking his knees so that his legs wouldn't tremble. When he was sure he was in complete control, he hurried back to the mouth of the cave.

Obi-Wan was sitting cross-legged in a meditation pose, waiting for him. Surprised, he rose to his feet when he saw Anakin.

"Are you real?" Anakin asked.

"Yes, I am real." Obi-Wan gripped Anakin's arm. "You see?"

Then he caught sight of the lightsaber. Anakin had deactivated it but held it loosely by his side. "What's this?" He held out a hand, and Anakin gave it to him. He gave Anakin an incredulous look. "You made this?"

"I . . . I must have," Anakin said. He did not want to tell Obi-Wan about his vision of the Sith. "You appeared to me. You told me to go into a trance state. I felt the Force very strongly."

Obi-Wan handed the lightsaber back to Anakin. "This is a good sign, Padawan. You let your feelings guide you. Look what you accomplished. When you allow your instincts to take over, they will not fail you. Remember in the battle of Naboo how you destroyed the Droid Control ship? The Force is always with you."

Anakin nodded. He took comfort from the pleasure and pride in Obi-Wan's voice. Every Jedi went through trials to build a lightsaber. He had overcome terrible visions. He had won. He would not think of the words that the Sith Lord had spoken.

Obi-Wan's comlink signaled. He spoke into it and listened intently. Then he cut the communication and turned to Anakin.

"We are wanted back at the Temple," he said. "The Council has a mission for us."

A mission! The thought crowded out the disturbing visions. Anakin sprang to his feet. He clipped his new lightsaber onto his belt. At last he could be a true partner to his Master. He would not think of his disturbing trance, the mystery of how the lightsaber was made. It did not matter. This lightsaber had made him a Jedi.

CHAPTER 4

"You're fidgeting," Obi-Wan told Anakin.

They stood outside the Jedi Council Room at the Temple. The small waiting area had comfortable seating, but Obi-Wan preferred to stand, and Anakin couldn't sit still. The minutes ticked by, and still they were not called.

"Why do you think Chancellor Palpatine will be in the meeting?" Anakin asked, taking in a slow, deep breath to still his muscles.

"I don't know."

"But you suspect."

"Speculation is a waste of time. Especially," Obi-Wan added, "when you are waiting for the Jedi Council."

"You sound like a droid," Anakin grumbled. "Can't you tell me how you feel?"

"I feel that you are overly anxious about this mission," Obi-Wan said.

Anakin fingered the new lightsaber by his side. He wasn't anxious, but he was impatient. Obviously, the presence of Chancellor Palpatine meant that the upcoming mission was a crucial one. Obi-Wan just didn't want to tell him so. The fact that they were chosen also had to mean that the hesitations that Anakin knew the Jedi Council still held about him must be fading.

The door to a conference room outside the Council Chamber swished open. Anakin's heart speeded up. *Don't fidget,* he warned himself as he stepped into the conference room.

Obi-Wan moved to the center of the room, and Anakin took his place by his Master's side. Members of the Jedi Council surrounded them in seating that conformed to height so that each Jedi had an equal view. The floor-to-ceiling windows presented a panoramic view of the busy sky lanes of Coruscant. Anakin had learned not to be distracted by his keen interest in the many sleek transports that zoomed by. Even the flicker of a glance could catch the disapproval of Mace Windu.

Chancellor Palpatine was standing near Mace

Windu. He wore a robe of rich, deep maroon in soft veda cloth. An ornate overcloak of blue swept the tips of his boots. Anakin was reassured to see a welcoming expression on his kindly face. The Chancellor nodded slightly in recognition. They had met on Naboo just after Anakin had been accepted for Jedi training.

"We have been asked by the Senate to undertake an escort mission," Mace Windu began. As usual, he did not waste time on preliminaries. "The Council has chosen you to accompany a Colicoid diplomatic ship."

"Dangerous, this mission will not be," Yoda said. "Yet delicate, it is."

Anakin suppressed a sigh. It wasn't that he hoped for danger, exactly. But a little excitement would be welcome.

"The Colicoids do not welcome the Jedi presence," Obi-Wan guessed. Anakin always admired how quickly his mind worked.

Yoda nodded. "Yet know it is necessary, they do."

"What is the threat to the ship?" Obi-Wan asked.

Chancellor Palpatine gave a quick look to Yoda to ask permission to speak. Yoda blinked his large eyes in agreement.

"The pirate Krayn is known to be in the area in which the Colicoids will be traveling," the Chancellor explained. "He's shown no hesitation in attacking diplomatic vessels in the past, but we think a Jedi team might be a deterrent." Palpatine shook his head gravely. "Krayn and his two associates, Rashtah and Zora, are ruthless. When Krayn hijacks ships, he not only steals their cargo, but sells their inhabitants into slavery."

Krayn. Anakin tightened his muscles. What was it about that name that caused his body to react with fear? He felt suddenly cold. Only the discipline he'd learned from Jedi training helped him suppress his body's involuntary shiver.

Krayn . . .

Slave trader. Slave raider.

The name on everyone's lips on that terrible day.

Raider, trader, raider, Anakin's brain chanted nonsensically. Remembering hovered above him, just out of reach. He could only feel the dread it would bring.

Then memory bloomed inside him. It filled his blood like a poison. Every detail rushed at him, just as he'd sworn to recall them that day.

He remembered the cool, crisp day on Tatooine. A picnic. Flowers woven through Amee's braids. The sweet taste of fruit pastry. And then the sudden shock of hurrying through their row of quarters, seeing faces unrecognizable from terrible fear . . .

He had burst into his quarters and seen his mother,

her legs tucked up against her chest, as if protecting herself from a blow. She had looked up and he had glimpsed terror on her face . . . *No! He had not meant to remember that!*

The cave! It had been a memory as well as a vision. Anakin understood that clearly now. The events clicked in with frightening vividness. He had suppressed the memory with an act of will. But he had not been able to shut it out forever.

Now memory had chosen to return at this moment, while members of the Jedi Council had their eyes on him. Anakin almost groaned aloud.

Obi-Wan sensed something. He shifted his weight slightly, drawing a bit closer to Anakin. The unspoken message was clear: *I am here, Anakin. Hang on.*

But Anakin was already conquering his shock. He told himself that he was *meant* to remember now, in this place. Shock hardened into resolve. He had felt Krayn in the cave. He might have been the figure chasing Shmi. Even though Anakin had never seen the pirate, he knew him. He knew the terror he had spread.

At last there was a chance he could face him. How lucky to have been given this assignment! His hand moved unconsciously to his lightsaber hilt.

"With all respect to the Council and the Senate,"

Obi-Wan said, "I am not certain that we are the correct team for this assignment."

Anakin could not resist an incredulous look at his Master. What was Obi-Wan doing? They were the perfect team for this assignment!

"The Council might recall that Anakin was once a slave himself," Obi-Wan continued. "He is sensitive to this issue. And as a young Padawan —"

"I am not too young!" Anakin broke in. "And I'm not too sensitive!"

Mace Windu fixed his dark gaze on Anakin, the forbidding look that could cause even a senior Jedi student to suddenly remember each tiny infraction of the rules he or she had committed since the age of five. "We will ask you to speak when we wish your opinion, Anakin."

Anakin was cowed by Mace Windu's reprimand. Mace Windu turned to Obi-Wan with the same severity.

"Do you have doubts about your Padawan, Obi-Wan? If so, you must state them. Certainly they are not obvious to the Council, since only recently you stood in that very spot and vehemently argued that he was ready for the trip to Ilum to fashion his own lightsaber."

So Obi-Wan had to fight to take him to Ilum. Defiance flared in Anakin. His chin lifted. So what? If the Council still had hesitations about him, they would soon learn differently.

"Please forgive me for interfering," Chancellor Palpatine interrupted softly. "I think I understand Obi-Wan Kenobi's hesitation. Even in my limited knowledge of Jedi procedures, I understand that Anakin Skywalker is a special case. Naturally the Jedi would wish to protect him more so than another Jedi student."

Anakin's face flushed. A special case! Needing protection! He felt humiliation wash over him.

"Anakin Skywalker is not a special case," Obi-Wan said in a firm voice. "Only his extraordinary abilities set him apart. He is certainly not in need of protection. Perhaps I expressed myself badly. I consider him fully able to conduct any mission the Council wishes to send him on. My hesitation was momentary. I accept the mission for myself and my Padawan."

Slowly, Mace Windu nodded. Yoda did as well, but his gaze lingered on Anakin.

Anakin didn't care. His Master had spoken up for him. They had a mission. Nothing else mattered. And there was a possibility he could meet Krayn face-to-face. That was the most important thing of all.

CHAPTER 5

The Colicoid ship was massive and utilitarian. Even the Colicoid diplomatic ships were pressed into service as cargo ships, and the planet's ship designers were known for ingenuity rather than style. They managed to pack more cargo space into a cruiser than anyone in the galaxy. They did this by compressing living space. Cabins and public areas were cramped and oddly shaped, mostly tucked into stray corners. It would not be a luxurious flight.

Luckily Obi-Wan had reached the point where he barely registered his surroundings, except as points of interest for the mission ahead. Anakin, however, was appalled at the sheer ugliness of the Colicoid transport. When it came to spaceships, Anakin was a firm believer in speed and elegance.

"I thought diplomatic ships were supposed to be the best in the planet's fleet," he murmured to

Obi-Wan as they boarded. They followed a guide down a narrow hallway, squeezing past equipment panels and cargo boxes.

"This *is* the best in the fleet," Obi-Wan murmured back.

They reached the bridge. The command center was smaller than it should be for a ship of this size. The pilot crew was jammed up against one another and the tech consoles. Even the ceiling was put into service for cargo — finely spun durasteel nets were suspended there and filled with cargo boxes. The full load blocked out the lighting from above, creating pools of shadow on the bridge. The total effect was one of deep gloom.

"Captain, the Jedi team has arrived," their guide reported.

The captain waved a long hand behind him but did not turn. "Dismissed."

The guide turned and left. The captain still ignored the Jedi. He stared down at a data screen mounted on the tech console.

Obi-Wan knew the Colicoids were barely tolerating their presence. If the captain wanted to play a game of patience with him, he would not engage. He cautioned Anakin with a look — he was not to betray any impatience. Anakin immediately composed his features and stilled a restless tapping finger on his utility belt. Obi-Wan could still tell his Padawan was restless, but the Colicoids would not.

The Colicoids were an intelligent species with armor-plated trunks, long, antennaed heads, and powerful stinging tails. Although renowned as deadly fighters, they had long ago turned their considerable energies toward trade. They had transferred their ruthlessness to commerce and were a wealthy species as a result.

The captain turned at last. His expression was not welcoming. He clicked two of his spidery legs together in impatience.

"I am Captain Anf Dec. We will be departing in six minutes," he said. "You are free to walk about the ship, but do not get in the way."

Obi-Wan matched the captain's brusque tone. "If any suspicious vessels enter our range, you will notify us?"

"No need for alarm. We do not expect trouble. Or so the Senate tells us." The captain gave an eerie smile that showed straight rows of sharp teeth. "The Jedi are aboard."

"Nevertheless, we expect to be notified if there is a potential problem," Obi-Wan said firmly.

The captain shrugged. "As you wish." The words came like explosive puffs of air. Obviously Captain Anf

Dec did not appreciate getting orders, only giving them. "Now go. We are busy."

Obi-Wan and Anakin turned and left the bridge.

"Friendly guy," Anakin said.

"I think it's best if we stay out of the Colicoids' way," Obi-Wan responded.

"No problem," Anakin muttered under his breath.

They proceeded to their cramped cabin, which they would have to share. Anakin placed his survival pack neatly by his narrow sleep-couch. Obi-Wan knew that his Padawan was still upset by the meeting at the Temple. Usually he would have to counsel Anakin at the start of a mission to settle down. The boy would run on an excess of energy and expectation and want to see everything at once. The Anakin he knew would have tossed his survival pack down and suggested a quick tour of the ship. But this new, silent Anakin merely sat on the sleep-couch and gazed at his surroundings with an uncurious eye.

Obi-Wan debated whether to speak. He knew what was bothering Anakin — the boy was troubled by both the Jedi Council's continuing wariness of his suitability and the implication that he was somehow different from other Jedi students. That did not worry Obi-Wan too much. He knew that Anakin's belief in himself was strong. Anakin *was* different, and he was learning that this was part of his strength. It did not have to set him apart. And Obi-Wan had told him before that he should not take the Council's rigor personally. It did not mean that they didn't think he would make a fine Jedi. It was their job to look for every possible trouble spot, to be harder on the Jedi students than their Masters would be. No doubt they, as well as he, had noticed Anakin's involuntary movement toward his lightsaber when slave trading was mentioned.

No, Anakin's silence was not about the Council's reaction, or Palpatine's words. He was hurt because Obi-Wan had tried to get out of the assignment. It suggested to his Padawan that he did not have faith in him — which was far from the truth.

Words that hurt were spoken in a moment. But words that heal take time and reflection.

Obi-Wan could not reassure Anakin that his words were spoken out of haste. He *was* worried about the effect of this mission on Anakin. If they did engage with Krayn, Anakin's deepest emotions would be tapped. Obi-Wan knew his Padawan had not begun to truly deal with the years of shame and anger he had passed as a slave. Someday he would confront this. Obi-Wan fervently wished that day to be in the future, after Anakin had honed his training.

Yet he had the feeling that this was exactly why

Mace Windu and Yoda had chosen them. It was not the first time Obi-Wan had suspected the Council of being too harsh.

They had suspended Obi-Wan once, taken away his Jedi status. He had been thirteen years old, and at the time he had not understood the Council's severity. He was forced to bypass his feelings to examine his own role in his suspension. He had been wrong, and he had come to understand that. The knowledge of this had shamed him. It was only through Qui-Gon's counsel that he had learned that his shame was preventing him from healing.

Could he teach his Padawan the same lesson? Qui-Gon had done it with a characteristic balance of severity and gentleness. No one mixed the two like his Master. Obi-Wan found it difficult to be severe with Anakin. He had been deeply influenced by his Master, but he was not Qui-Gon. He would have to find his own way.

The Master must guard against guiding the Padawan according to his own needs. He or she must balance care and discipline with the acknowledgment of the Padawan's separateness, his or her distinct character.

Qui-Gon's caution had chafed Obi-Wan at times. Now he completely understood it. The shadow of Xanatos had always stood at Qui-Gon's shoulder. Xanatos had been Qui-Gon's Padawan, and he had turned to the dark side. Qui-Gon had struggled to keep Obi-Wan and Xanatos separate in his mind and actions. He did not want his training of Obi-Wan to be haunted by the ways he might have failed Xanatos. But it was not always easy. Of course Qui-Gon and Obi-Wan had gone on to build a rich history together. Obi-Wan wished the same fierce trust and affection between himself and Anakin. They had already begun to build it.

"I received more information about Krayn before we left," Obi-Wan told Anakin. "You should review this file." He called up the information on his datapad and handed it to Anakin.

"There is a profile of Krayn's ship and his illegal activities as well as background on his two associates. One is a Wookiee named Rashtah. Very fierce, very dangerous. Unusual for a Wookiee to be involved in slave trading, but he's extremely loyal to Krayn. There's another associate called Zora, a human female."

Anakin flipped through the holographic file. "There's not much information here on her."

"No. She joined Krayn about a year ago." Obi-Wan turned away. He knew all about Zora. Yoda and Mace Windu had briefed him privately before he left. Anakin did not have to know yet that Zora was a former Jedi.

More important, Zora was a former friend of Obi-Wan's. Her former name was Siri. She had been in Temple training with Obi-Wan, just a year behind. He had known her well, or as well as anyone could know her. Her deepest emotions were known only to herself. The two of them had been on missions together as Padawans. Chosen by Council member Adi Gallia as an apprentice, Siri had been acutely intelligent and scrupulously mindful of Jedi rules.

Her loyalty to Adi Gallia was unquestioned . . . until they had fallen into a severe disagreement. Adi Gallia was known for her intuition, but not necessarily her warmth. She had taken the most severe path a Master could — she had cut loose her Padawan without recommending her for full Jedi status. Furious, Siri had left the Temple abruptly. Obi-Wan had tried to find her, but she had cut off any contact with the Temple. She had wandered the galaxy. Without her Jedi family, without any ties, she had fallen into bad company. And now she was using her skills to work with Krayn. It was an astonishing transformation, but Qui-Gon had taught Obi-Wan that he should not be surprised by the dark forces that battled within every being. Siri had battled her dark side and lost.

Obi-Wan and Anakin felt the engines thrum underneath their feet. The ship slowly rose from its docking port, then shot out into a space lane. Soon they would be far above Coruscant, engaging the hyperdrive.

"Do you think Krayn will attack the ship?" Anakin asked, looking out at the sky through the small viewport.

"The Colicoids don't seem to think so," Obi-Wan said. "Who knows? Krayn has a complicated, galaxy-wide operation. He might not want the trouble of tangling with Jedi."

There was something like disappointment on Anakin's face. *He* wants *to meet up with Krayn,* Obi-Wan realized. It was probably the normal reaction of a young man longing for adventure. Or it could be something darker.

"You seemed to react to Krayn's name during the briefing," Obi-Wan said. "Have you heard of him?"

Anakin turned his gaze back to Obi-Wan. There was the trace of a shadow in his eyes, something that only Obi-Wan would notice, he felt sure. "I know his kind."

He was holding something back. He had not really answered Obi-Wan's question. Anakin never lied to him. Obi-Wan realized with a deep sense of unease that he was lying now.

CHAPTER 6

"Don't touch that!" A Colicoid officer scurried for-ward, legs clicking. Anakin stepped back from the equipment console in the tech readout room. They were coming out of hyperspace too soon.

"I wasn't touching it," Anakin said. "I was just looking at it. I've never seen a tech console like this before."

"Well, go away," the officer said, blocking the tech console. "This is not a place for little boys."

Anakin drew his power around him. He knew it was there, a combination of his own will and the Force, easily tapped, always reachable. He fixed his gaze on the officer. "I am not a little boy. I am a Jedi."

The Colicoid was clearly unnerved as the young human boy before him gave him a gaze of such con-centrated intensity. It took all of his will to stand his ground.

"Well, go away anyway," he muttered, turning away from that unsettling look. "This is no place for you."

Anakin decided instantly that the tech console was not interesting enough to risk a confrontation. He walked away with a dignity that masked his irritation. The Colicoids were certainly touchy about their ship. In his experience, most beings were happy to indulge in tech-talk and were proud of their ships. The Colicoids didn't seem to bond with their transports, just looked at them as a way to get them from one place to another. Normally he would fill his time poking into the ship's nooks and crannies, but the Colicoid crew was constantly breathing down his neck.

He never knew a mission could be so boring.

If only Krayn would attack!

Anakin stopped, appalled at the thought that had risen so buoyantly into his mind. Jedi did not wish for confrontation, but met it squarely when it came. They looked for peaceful outcomes. He should not long for a pirate invasion to spice up a dull trip. It was as wrong as wrong could be.

But to be fair, he didn't want Krayn to attack because he was bored. The thought of the pirate was like a fever in his blood. He wanted — *needed* — to see Krayn face-to-face. He wanted to know if the vision he'd had in the cave was true.

He still felt guilty about lying to Obi-Wan. He could not tell Obi-Wan how memory had burst inside him, a burning memory full of details that were as fresh and painful as they'd been six years before.

Well, he hadn't exactly lied — he simply hadn't given a full answer. Unfortunately, to the Jedi, that was the same as lying to a Master. Sometimes the strict Jedi scruples could be extremely annoying.

He could not speak of Krayn. Not yet. If he spoke the memory aloud, it would choke him. He was afraid of the emptiness he felt whenever he remembered his mother. There were so many sleepless nights when he berated himself for the comfort of his sleep-couch at the Temple, for his plentiful meals, his excellent education, but mostly, for his happiness there. How could he continue to take even one more contented breath when his mother languished as a slave on a desolate planet?

In the beginning, when he'd first arrived at the Temple, he could call up her voice and smile so easily. He could repeat her soft words to him: *The greatest gift you can give me, Annie, is to take your freedom.*

But her voice was growing fainter, and her smile growing dim. Sometimes he had to struggle to recall the living reality of her face, the texture of her skin. He had not seen her in four years. He had been so young when he left. His greatest fear was that one day she would leave him completely. That he would lose her like a dream. Then he would be hollow inside.

Obi-Wan Kenobi had been raised in the Temple since he was a baby. He could not truly know how a childhood could be one of terror and shame mixed with comfort and love. He only knew this through his intellect, not his experience. It is one thing to see the effects of a terrible childhood. It is another to live them every day. So when his beloved Master told him he must accept his anger and let it move through him, a small, mean voice in Anakin whispered that his Master did not know what he was talking about. He did not truly know anger.

How could he let such rage move through him? Obi-Wan could never understand how it beat inside him, threatening never to leave. It had the power to consume him. It frightened him, and Anakin did not want to accept fear, either. Did this mean he could never be a Jedi Knight?

When he thought of his fears, his thoughts circled in just this way, bringing a spark of panic deep in his belly. It was better to pretend the anger wasn't there. Wasn't being a Jedi all about control? He had to find his own way to control his feelings. That would be the best way.

Suddenly, Anakin felt a tremor in the ship. It caused him to stumble slightly. The tremor was followed by a blast that sent him flying into the corridor wall. Alarm signals began to sound.

Anakin took off through the maze of twisting corridors toward his quarters to find Obi-Wan. The ship was hit again by another blast, and began to practice defensive maneuvers. Anakin knew the ship was too large to outmaneuver most crafts.

He was halfway there when he saw Obi-Wan running toward him.

"We're under attack. It's Krayn," Obi-Wan said tersely. "Let's head for the bridge."

CHAPTER 7

The two raced into the gloom of the bridge. The crew sat tensely at the controls while a few officers raced from one station to another. Outside the view-port, they could see vapor trails of proton torpedoes and showers of explosives. The ship shook with every nearby blast. It was an ambush — Krayn must have known where they would appear.

Captain Anf Dec stood, his hands gripping the arms of his control chair. "Where is the ship?" he screamed. "Where is the ship?"

"It dived below us, Captain," one of the crew members shouted.

"Full speed ahead! Full speed! No, left engines full!" Captain Anf Dec shouted, his voice on the edge of hysteria. "Where is the ship now?"

The ship lurched to one side as the crew struggled to reconcile the captain's contradictory orders. This

lurch was followed by another blast that sent everyone on the bridge staggering.

"Krayn is off to our port, sir," one of the crew
members said. "We've taken a blow to the fuel
driver."

"What is he doing!" Captain Anf Dec shouted.
"Doesn't he know who we are?"

"Yes, Captain. We informed the ship that we were
a Colicoid ship with a Jedi observation team aboard.
As per your instructions," the crew member added
pointedly.

"Port-side deflector shield is down," another crew
member shouted.

"What?" the captain asked, scuttling over to stare
at the readout. "How could that be?"

"We didn't get it fully operational in time —"

"Idiots!" Captain Anf Dec nearly fell over as another
blast shook the ship. "It's an ambush — they must
have reset the coordinates of our nav computer."

Anakin and Obi-Wan stared out the viewport as the
pirate ship shot into view. It was smaller than the Colicoid transport, but highly maneuverable. By the look
of the orbital gun platforms and laser cannons, they
were also vastly outgunned.

Because of his acute connection to the Force,
Anakin knew his ability to read situations was far-

ranging. He didn't need the Force now to tell him that with a failing ship and a panicked captain, they were in trouble. If they couldn't outmaneuver Krayn or out-run him, what options were left? He looked at his Master. When it came to strategic thinking, he de-pended on Obi-Wan. His Master could not only process all aspects of difficult situations, he could come up with several strategies and hone in on the best one — all within seconds.

"Our only hope is to get a small transport off this ship and infiltrate Krayn's ship," Obi-Wan said. "If we can get aboard, we could disable the weapons sys-tem."

"What's that?" The Colicoid captain turned his long head. "What did you say?"

"Will you authorize release of one of your trans-ports to us?" Obi-Wan asked.

"What for?"

"To infiltrate Krayn's ship," Obi-Wan repeated. "It's the only way we'll escape destruction or cap-ture."

"Do what you want. I don't care." Captain Anf Dec clutched the arms of his chair as the ship lurched from another blow. "Just do something!"

"We'll need you to create a diversion."

"Fine!"

Without another word, Obi-Wan turned and ran off the bridge. Anakin followed, his heart racing. He admired how his Master had sized up the situation and chosen a course of action within seconds. It was a daring move, but it could be their only hope.

They reached the cargo bay doors, where a number of small transports sat. They were used to ferry passengers or cargo to and from the surface while the large ship orbited a planet.

Obi-Wan stopped and turned to Anakin. "Choose."

Gratified by his Master's trust, Anakin turned to the ships. He surveyed them with a pilot's eye, but also drew in the Force to help with the decision. He needed to go on instinct now. He trusted that it would tell him the right ship to choose.

"The G-class shuttle," he said to Obi-Wan.

Obi-Wan hesitated. "The lighter could be faster."

Anakin grinned. "Not the way I fly."

Obi-Wan nodded. They ran toward the three-winged shuttle. Anakin activated the hatch and swung himself up into the cockpit. Obi-Wan followed.

Quickly, Anakin familiarized himself with the controls. There wasn't a ship made that he couldn't fly. He contacted the crew who operated the bay doors and quickly instructed them that they had Captain Anf Dec's permission to leave. After a moment, the doors opened slightly, and Anakin activated the two lower wings, which lifted into flight mode. They blasted off into space.

"There," Obi-Wan said after only a few seconds. "If you can keep near his exhaust, I think our ship is small enough to escape detection. Not to mention that Krayn has other things on his mind." The Colicoid had kept his promise to create a diversion, flying erratically and letting off enough fire to keep Krayn occupied.

"And what should I do then?" Anakin asked.

"I'm open to suggestions," Obi-Wan answered.

But Anakin's mind was already working as soon as Obi-Wan said "exhaust." If they could hug the rear of the pirate ship, they might be able to slip into the exhaust system. The steam would overheat the craft, but if Anakin could push the ship fast enough, they might be able to make it into the interior.

Quickly, he described his plan to Obi-Wan.

Obi-Wan nodded. "It's possible. But the exhaust tunnels narrow as they travel inside the ship. We could be trapped."

"That's why this shuttle will come in handy," Anakin said. "I can retract the wings by degrees and use the third wing to fly."

Obi-Wan frowned. "That will give you less control."

Anakin nodded. "I know."

"And the heat will be intense in that shaft. The ship could overheat."

"Not if I speed." Anakin knew what Obi-Wan was thinking. He would have to pilot the ship fast enough to escape overheating, yet not so fast that he'd lose his maneuverability. "I think I can manage it."

"You think?"

"I *know*."

"Fine. Let's do it."

Krayn's ship had not spotted them, and Anakin was able to precisely mirror the pirate ship's quick attack maneuvers. By hugging Krayn's stern, he was able to escape detection. He anticipated which way the ship would move as it attacked again and again at the vulnerable parts of the Colicoid ship. He followed the ship like a shadow, all the time easing closer to the great exhaust valve at the stern.

The exhaust valve contained a huge whirring propeller. Anakin hung in the air, his fingers on the controls, timing the propeller's turn. Obi-Wan remained silent, allowing Anakin to gather his concentration. The tiniest miscalculation could send them into the twirling blades.

Anakin knew the seconds were ticking away, and

he appreciated Obi-Wan's silence. He waited until the Force gathered and united with his instincts and perceptions. He fixed his gaze on the spinning blades. They seemed to slow with the level of his concentration. As soon as he felt sure that he had fully absorbed the rhythm, he pushed the engines and felt the craft zoom toward the exhaust port. He flipped the shuttle sideways to slip through the blades.

The small craft shuddered from the wind created by the powerful blades, but it zoomed through an opening with only centimeters to spare. Anakin kept his hands tight on the controls. Suddenly there was a blast of energy from the powerful exhaust. He was being pushed back into the blades again!

"Hold on!" he shouted.

He pushed the throttle forward, giving it all he had. A simple touch of the blade would send the ship spiraling out of control.

The engines kicked in. Anakin had to struggle to keep the ship steady.

They were speeding now — *too fast.* Within seconds, he saw that Obi-Wan had been correct. The shaft was narrowing. Soon there were only a few meters between the wings and the sides of the tunnel. Anakin quickly activated the wing controls so that the two side wings folded up toward the body of the ship. He felt the controls jump in his hands, but he held the ship firmly, slowing it down.

"I see light ahead," Obi-Wan murmured. Although Anakin knew there would be no censure in his Master's voice, he knew he'd cut it too close this time. Obi-Wan continued, "I'm betting we'll come out near the turbine in the power core. I hope there's room to land."

So did Anakin. The ship was now bumping with the fierce air currents, and he bent his will toward gentling it like a skittish bantha. Between the wing instability and the power of the exhaust, the ship was close to losing control.

But it wouldn't. He wouldn't allow it. He trusted in the ship's ability to take them where they needed to go.

He powered down the engines slightly as the shaft narrowed. They burst through the opening into the central power core. Anakin quickly avoided the giant turbines that sent energy blasts and steam down the shaft. If he landed directly in front of the exhaust shaft and turned off the engines, a good blast from the exhaust could send the ship back into the blades. Instead he eased the shuttle craft down in the tiny space nearby. It was still close to the shaft, but the exhaust was not powerful enough to move the ship. He set the landing gear to lock.

Obi-Wan scanned the area. "Let's make for that catwalk. It will most likely lead to some sort of tech station. The ship is in attack mode, so the crew will be too busy to notice us. Let's hope so, anyway."

Anakin opened the hatch and they climbed down from the ship. Immediately they were hit with a staggering blast of heat. Ignoring it, they ran lightly toward the catwalk. Accessing the Force, they leaped over the railing high above. Then they ran down the twisting metal walk past the giant generators.

The catwalk led to a small door that had a small wheel that served as a manual opening device. Obi-Wan quickly twisted the wheel one full revolution. His hand on his lightsaber hilt, he went through the door.

They were in a tech readout room for the power core. It was empty. These readouts were backups, used only for emergencies. Obi-Wan proceeded to another door and accessed it. This time, they found themselves in a narrow, grimy hallway.

"We have to search for the weapons control tech center," Obi-Wan murmured. "It must be nearby. We can't expect it to be empty, however. On the contrary."

Anakin followed Obi-Wan down the hallway. Moving fast, they came to the end of the corridor. A window in the wide double door showed them the interior of a tech center. Obi-Wan motioned to Anakin to stay on one side of the door. He peered through the window. Everyone was too busy to notice him.

The center was staffed by tech droids. Since the weaponry was controlled at the bridge, the droids were merely monitoring the different systems.

"The droids are equipped with arm and chest blasters," he told Anakin. "No doubt they are programmed to kill anyone who interferes with the control panels. We'll only have a few seconds before they register our presence as threatening. There are fourteen of them."

Anakin nodded. He withdrew his lightsaber. "Ready."

Obi-Wan opened the door and walked into the room, Anakin at his heels.

"Inspection," he announced.

A droid who was patrolling the others turned its rotating head. "Authorization?"

Obi-Wan's lightsaber glowed. "Here."

He sprang forward, slicing toward the control panel. At the same time, Anakin moved to the left to take out the patrolling droid. He neatly sliced the head off the droid, which wobbled, arms waving, until he buried his lightsaber in its chest control panel. He felt a surge of satisfaction from the power of his new lightsaber. He wasn't in training mode anymore.

The other droids were quick. They swiveled in their stools and rose as one, blaster fire pinging from their chests and arms.

The blaster fire sang in Anakin's ears, random and close. The room was small and bare. There wasn't space to evade fire, and nowhere to hide. The two Jedi had to rely on their lightsabers only.

Anakin kept his lightsaber moving, trying to deflect fire as he moved forward. The perfect balance of the lightsaber helped his accuracy and speed. He kicked out with one leg and sent a droid flying, then somersaulted toward another, cleaving off one blaster arm and then slicing the droid in two. On his downswing, he demolished the droid on the floor for good. Turning, he went for the third droid.

Obi-Wan was a blur. He whirled, dived, leaped, and kicked, his lightsaber constantly moving. He held out a hand and the Force blasted a droid against the wall. Within seconds, he had demolished seven droids and turned to help Anakin reduce the last droid to a smoking heap on the floor.

"Now for the weapons system," he said.

"Do you know how to disable it?" Anakin asked.

Obi-Wan grinned. "Sure. I'll use a trick Qui-Gon taught me." He raised his lightsaber overhead and then slashed down onto the control panel. Smoke rose and metal sizzled. He aimed a second blow, then a third. Soon the control panel was completely demolished.

"That should do it. Let's go."

Anakin hurried after Obi-Wan. He knew they had only seconds before more droids arrived.

Obi-Wan started down the long hallway back toward the power core. Anakin suddenly halted.

It didn't feel right to him to leave the ship. Krayn was here, within their grasp. They had a chance to annihilate a vicious slave trader who had imprisoned thousands and was responsible for the deaths of countless innocent beings.

How could they leave?

At the end of the corridor, Obi-Wan sensed that Anakin was not behind him. He turned. "What is it?"

"I can't leave." Anakin shook his head firmly. "We aren't finished. We have to destroy Krayn."

"That is not our mission, Anakin —"

Grimly, Anakin turned away. "It's mine."

He turned in the opposite direction from Obi-Wan and began to run.

CHAPTER 8

Shocked, Obi-Wan couldn't move for a moment. Anakin had caught him completely off balance. He hadn't seen this coming.

He should have.

Obi-Wan wheeled around and charged after his Padawan. Anakin had taken the corridor off the weapons tech center. The corridor was already empty as Obi-Wan raced down it. After a few steps it opened onto a hallway with four branches of corridors. Anakin wasn't visible down any of them.

Obi-Wan gritted his teeth in annoyance. Any moment now some sort of squad would check on those droids. As soon as they entered that readout room, they'd know that there were saboteurs aboard the ship. A general alarm would be issued. In the meantime, the Colicoid ship might be defeated. He had to find Anakin, and fast.

He reached out with the Force, searching the energy around him for Anakin. But the ship was too large and crammed with beings. Too much dark energy swirled around, acting like a veil between the Jedi. Not to mention that Anakin himself did not want to be found.

With nothing else to do, Obi-Wan took the first corridor on his right.

Obviously, the pirate Krayn did not care about cleanliness aboard his ship. While the Colicoid ship was cramped, it was relatively clean. Krayn's ship was littered with debris and the walls and floor were sticky with grime and oil. Whenever Obi-Wan heard footsteps he quickly ducked into one of the small cargo rooms that led off the corridors.

But time was running out, and he had to quicken his pace and rely on his lightsaber to get him out of trouble. Obi-Wan followed the corridor, being careful to keep his sense of direction. All the corridors seemed to twist around each other and intersect at the central point where he'd started. It was like searching a maze.

He was exploring the third corridor, running as fast as he dared, when he heard the unmistakable quick metallic steps of a troop of attack droids. Obi-Wan had only seconds to decide whether to engage them or run. With Anakin still on the loose, he chose to double back and duck into the adjacent corridor.

But this one wasn't empty. It was full of pirates.

There were at least twenty of them. They were just as surprised as he was and fumbled for their weapons. Obi-Wan leaped forward, activating his lightsaber, ready for the first assault.

As the pirates registered his lightsaber, they seemed stunned. To Obi-Wan's surprise, a group in front slowly lowered their weapons. Every pirate in the room followed, laying his or her weapon on the floor.

One of the pirates stepped forward. Obi-Wan noted that his tunic was almost in rags.

"We are at your mercy, Jedi," he said.

Warily, Obi-Wan kept his lightsaber activated.

The pirate spoke in a hushed tone. "I am Condi, from the planet Zoraster. I am not a pirate. I am a slave. As are my companions. Stolen from our home worlds by Krayn. Under penalty of death, we have been assigned guard duty aboard the ship." Condi looked at him eagerly. "Thank the moons and stars, we have rescue in our grasp at last."

Obi-Wan deactivated his lightsaber. The naked desperation on Condi's face unnerved him. It was mirrored in the faces of his companions. All of them had obviously suffered great deprivations.

"I am sorry," he said. "I have not come on a rescue mission."

Condi's face fell, then brightened. "But you can take us with you. We will help you fight."

"I cannot." Obi-Wan felt these two words were the most difficult he had ever said. "I have only a small ship, big enough for me and my companion." He wanted to promise them he would return, but how could he make that promise? If he got off the ship safely with Anakin, Krayn would be gone. The ship could hide anywhere in the galaxy. He believed too strongly in a Jedi promise to make one he did not know if he could fulfill.

Someone spoke from the back. "So you leave us here, like this?"

Obi-Wan did not know how to answer. "I will do my best to help you," he finally said. "But not here. Not now. In order to help you, I must get off this ship."

Condi swallowed. "Then we will help you."

"No." Obi-Wan shook his head firmly. "That I will not allow. It will put you in danger. The best thing we can do for each other is part ways here."

Condi's face was full of anguish, but he nodded with dignity. "We have never seen you, Jedi."

"Thank you." Obi-Wan caught a flicker of movement at the end of the corridor. Anakin!

He raced through the slaves and toward his Padawan. Anakin saw him and stopped. He knew better than to run.

Obi-Wan came up. "Anakin, I have no time to argue with you. We must go."

"There are patrols everywhere," Anakin told him. "I can't find Krayn."

"Our best chance to destroy this operation is to leave this ship at once," Obi-Wan told him urgently.

"But he's here, now!" Anakin argued. "We can destroy him."

"Marking a being for death is not the Jedi way," Obi-Wan told him severely.

"Even when that being enslaves others, kills them as if they were nothing, imprisons them against their will?" Anakin argued. "I heard the slaves beg you to help them. I saw you turn your back on them. How can you abandon them to such misery? Every day for a slave is another chance to die. Killing Krayn will free them. How can you do this?"

"Anakin, you must be logical," Obi-Wan said, struggling to hold on to his composure. "How can I help them? If we want to bring down Krayn's empire, we must have a plan. We can't just sneak aboard his ship and hope to run into him."

"It seems as good a plan as any."

"It's not. And it could result in our deaths, and the deaths of many. If one miscalculation or mistake on our part occurs, Krayn will take his revenge on those he controls — the slaves. Our best plan is to leave now and get the Council to pledge their resources to bring down Krayn. There will be no more arguments here. Time is running out. Guards are most likely searching for us now, and I don't think the Colicoids will wait for our return much longer. Now come. You must understand that this is the best way."

"*You're* the one who doesn't understand!" Anakin shouted.

Obi-Wan was startled at Anakin's vehemence, but he kept his gaze on him, willing him to obey.

Anakin hesitated. He cast his eyes down sullenly. He would not disobey a direct order. Reluctantly, he nodded. Obi-Wan could tell that fury and frustration boiled within him.

They would need time to sort this out. Time they would have back aboard the Colicoid ship.

Obi-Wan did not have to turn and check to make sure that Anakin was behind him. He felt his furious resentment all the way back to the central power core. They did not meet any droid patrols and were able to sneak inside the power core once again. They hurried down the catwalk, running now.

Obi-Wan ducked under their transport, released the hatch, and climbed inside. He strapped himself into the pilot seat and signaled Anakin through the viewport to follow.

Anakin began to duck underneath the rim of the ship. Suddenly, blaster fire peppered the side of the ship near his head. Anakin ducked to the ground.

A pirate leaped off the catwalk, blasters in both hands. He looked human, and Obi-Wan fleetingly wondered how he could jump such a distance.

The pirate landed just a few feet from Anakin. He kept his blasters level but did not shoot again. His short hair was braided and studded with sharp glittering objects woven through the twisted strands. Various lethal weapons hung from his thick utility belt. He looked strong, but he wasn't very large.

Suddenly Obi-Wan realized that the pirate was a woman. Then familiar blue eyes flashed, and shock shimmered inside him.

This wasn't just a woman. The pirate was Siri.

CHAPTER 9

Siri no longer looked like a Jedi. She was dressed in a tunic and leggings fashioned from various skins. Blast padding covered her shoulders and chest. On her pale cheeks were red scars that on closer inspection he realized were facial markings designed to give her a fierce appearance. Her bright blond hair was darkened with some kind of grease. Obi-Wan was shocked by her savage appearance.

Yet he had to trust that she would not fire on Anakin.

"Anakin, get in," he called.

Anakin eyed Siri's blasters.

"You won't shoot him, Siri," Obi-Wan said.

"I am Siri no longer," Siri answered. "I am Zora."

"There is still Jedi in you," Obi-Wan said, "even though you have betrayed every part of our code."

"There are so many things I do not miss about the

Jedi," Siri said thoughtfully, blocking Anakin from the ship. "One is their self-righteousness. It's so boring."

Anakin gazed from Obi-Wan back to Siri, amazement on his face.

"Zora!" A huge, bellowing voice filled the space. "Did you find the intruders?"

"Krayn," Anakin said, even though no one was in sight yet.

"Get in!" Obi-Wan hissed.

"Zora!" The bellow was loud and close.

Siri sprang forward. With one sweeping motion, she closed the hatch, separating Anakin from Obi-Wan. Then she spun sideways toward the giant turbines. She accessed the control panel and pressed several buttons. The giant turbines began to spin faster.

Obi-Wan guessed her strategy a few seconds too late. He just had time to grab the controls when the turbines roared to life at three times their normal speed. A gust of wind picked the craft up like a feather and hurled it toward the shaft.

Fighting for control, Obi-Wan struggled to hold the ship steady. It crashed against one wall of the shaft, then smashed against the other side. He quickly opened the side wings slightly for more control. It wasn't easy to prevent the ship from crashing and burning in the narrow shaft, but he managed to keep it heading down the middle as it lurched.

The turning propellers ahead reminded him that he could be cut to bits. Obi-Wan drew on the Force, concentrating all his will on the task ahead. Time seemed to slow as he gauged his own speed and the speed of the powerful rotors. At the last possible second, he activated the wings fully and flipped sideways. As the ship slipped through the rotors, one of them clipped a wing. Spiraling crazily, the ship shot out into space.

Obi-Wan fought for control. He activated the third wing to take up some of the control he had lost. The ship slowly steadied beneath his hands. He cut back the engines and spun the craft around. Should he follow the ship, or attempt another landing inside the exhaust shaft? He asked himself the question, but he knew the ship did not have the control necessary to navigate that shaft again.

He couldn't leave Anakin to be captured by Siri and Krayn. He could not allow his Padawan to become a slave once again.

Then as he watched, Krayn's ship blasted into hyperspace in a shower of light energy.

He could not follow. His Padawan was gone.

CHAPTER 10

Everything had happened so fast. It was rare for Anakin to be caught by surprise. One moment he had been furious at Obi-Wan but ready to board the ship, and the next moment his Master was being blasted down the shaft. His Jedi reflexes still needed honing. Siri-Zora had completely turned the situation around while he was still absorbing what was happening.

Krayn appeared on the catwalk above.

Krayn was humanoid, but had the size and heft of a natural formation, a boulder, a tree. His body seemed carved out of rock. His shaved head glinted in the dim light. As he drew closer Anakin could see various items hanging from the double utility belt he had slung around his waist. They swung with the motion of his walk. He clutched a vibro-ax in one meaty fist, and his small, glittering eyes swept the scene before him with shrewdness.

A huge Wookiee stood by his side. Anakin realized this must be Rashtah. Ammunition belts crisscrossed his hairy body and a row of blasters were strapped to his waist. A jagged scar began under the hair of his scalp and traveled through his eye down to his lip. An eye patch covered that eye, hiding the damage. Rashtah waved his vibrosword at Siri and sent his own bellow of greeting.

Siri reached over and powered down the turbines. Anakin wondered what his best move would be. There was no game plan for this particular situation. Would the Siri part of Zora cover for him, or would the heartless-seeming Zora give him up immediately? She had certainly acted ruthlessly in the case of Obi-Wan.

His instincts flared. *Stay silent. Let her speak.*

So Anakin said nothing as Krayn stomped toward them, the vibro-ax twirling like a child's toy in his other hand.

"What's this? Have you caught our intruder?"

"No. This is nobody, just a slave," Siri said. "I grabbed him as a shield just in case, but he wasn't needed. I'm afraid our intruders took the exhaust tunnel back into space."

"If they made it." Krayn's dark eyes glittered. "I

gave the order to jump to hyperspace. If they were in the shaft when that happened, they're space dust."

The Wookiee gave a sound of amusement.

"That would be a bonus," Siri said. Her eyes glinted with the same cruelty as Krayn's.

She hates Obi-Wan, Anakin realized.

Krayn stuck his head closer to the exhaust shaft. "We'll have to figure out a way to block this from airships. Don't want to be surprised again. Heads will roll about this one."

While Krayn's back was to them and Rashtah was distracted, Siri reached over and deftly removed Anakin's lightsaber from his utility belt. Again, she had been quicker than his perception. She did it so quickly and smoothly that he barely registered that he had been disarmed. She thrust the lightsaber inside her tunic in the same smooth motion.

Krayn turned and gave his full attention to Anakin. Anakin met his gaze squarely. He could imagine that Krayn's gaze had the power to terrify, but it did not work on him. He was curious and contemptuous, not scared.

"What are you looking at, slave?" Krayn suddenly bellowed, his voice full of rage.

Anakin realized too late that slaves did not look directly at their masters. He had never been particularly good at submissive poses, anyway.

Siri lashed out with one leg, twisting it around his so that he was forced to stumble.

"Show some respect," she hissed.

Anakin gave her a look of pure loathing, but Krayn could not see it. He kept his eyes at mid-level when he turned back to Krayn.

"He looks strong," Krayn said, stroking his neatly trimmed black beard. "Should fetch a good price on Nar Shaddaa."

Now that his gaze was mid-level, Anakin realized that the objects dangling from Krayn's belt were talismans. They were objects Anakin didn't want to think about, for some of them resembled dried flesh and he could pick out bits of hair. There were jewels and crystals as well, and a small silver bell . . .

The silver bell. Anakin's gaze was riveted on it. He knew it. He recognized it. It was the bell that Amee's mother had worn around her neck.

Suddenly Krayn's meaty hand reached down and jangled some of the hanging items. The bell tinkled softly, and a strange pain seared Anakin's heart.

"Admiring my kill trophies?" Krayn asked him in a low, cunning tone. "Or do you think you might snatch a jewel or two? Think again, slave. One of your fingers or your scalp will end up hanging alongside them!"

He laughed, and Siri and Rashtah joined him. As Krayn shook with amusement, Anakin heard the tinkling of the bell. So Hala was dead. The sweet sound of the bell mingled with Krayn's harsh laughter until Anakin's vision blurred with rage. He could kill him, right here, right now. He would not need his lightsaber. He could do it with his bare hands. . . .

"I'd better get the slaves ready for departure," Siri said. "We'll be at Nar Shaddaa soon. Come, slave."

She prodded Anakin with the butt of her electrojabber. "Might as well enjoy the ship while you can. Soon you'll be working in the spice mines."

"For the rest of your life," Krayn added, still laughing.

Anakin felt his feet move as Siri prodded him again, this time more sharply. Krayn had not frightened him. Siri had not frightened him. The fact that he was alone had not frightened him.

But soon he would be sold again into slavery. He knew firsthand how hard it was for a slave to escape. He had heard tales of the spice mines and the mortality rate of the workers there. He knew how dreams of escape would color his days. He knew how one gray day would follow one gray day, where he would not lift his head but keep it bowed to work. He knew that the dull drudgery of his days would fill his soul until the dreams of escape flattened into a haze of numbing routine.

He thought he had faced his worst fear in the cave on Ilum. He had not. He realized now that he had just begun to taste it.

CHAPTER 11

Obi-Wan knew that it was useless for him to replay the situation, but he knew that if he had reacted faster, had jumped off the ship to confront Siri, he would not be in this position. His shock had slowed his reflexes. If Siri had been an ordinary enemy, he would not have been frozen in that pilot seat. If he had not remembered what she had been when she'd been his friend, he would not have imagined that she was capable of blasting him off the ship and taking Anakin as her captive.

Obi-Wan paced back and forth on the bridge of the Colicoid ship. He knew he was lucky to be there at all. He doubted the Colicoids would have waited for him if their own ship had not been damaged.

Captain Anf Dec had not bothered to hide the fact that he now considered the Jedi a nuisance. He did not even thank Obi-Wan for dismantling the weapons system of Krayn's ship, but indicated that it was the least the Jedi could do. Obi-Wan sensed that the captain was nervous about the reaction of his superiors to the mission. The Colicoids did not allow failure in their higher personnel.

He knew it was fruitless to track a ship through hyperspace, but he had demanded that the Colicoid communication system search the galaxy for possible exit vectors for Krayn's ship. He had to pressure Anf Dec with the full weight of the Senate and the Jedi Council before the captain agreed.

Of course the odds were stacked against him. A pirate ship did not register with host planets. If it needed repairs or supplies it went to a number of spaceports willing to make a few credits by catering to illegals, or simply captured a nearby unlucky vessel for parts or fuel.

Maybe, Obi-Wan thought, that was why Krayn had attacked them in the first place. Perhaps it was a simple mistake. If that were the case, Krayn was in need of fuel or supplies, and could be heading to the nearest spaceport that would accommodate an illegal.

So far the Colicoid search had turned up nothing.

But did Krayn make mistakes? Obi-Wan kept circling back to that question. From everything he'd read and seen in Krayn's data file, the pirate had managed to survive and thrive when his fellow criminals died in strategic miscalculations, private battles, and ill-judged alliances. Krayn was a despicable life-form, but he had intelligence and cunning.

Obi-Wan stopped pacing. He was allowing his worry over Anakin and disgust at himself to agitate him. When the body was agitated, the mind was as well.

He went still. He breathed. He found the place inside himself that knew second-guessing was a waste of time. He had done his best, made the calculations that he could. Any more recriminations would only slow him down.

As he reached into himself, Qui-Gon's words floated to the surface. His Master had often said them when they had reached what appeared to be a dead end in a mission.

Let's look at the who. That will lead us to the why.

He found his gaze resting on Captain Anf Dec. The captain's determined unfriendliness did not bother him. But other things did. As Obi-Wan tapped his instincts, he also uncovered a memory. He recalled his unease with Captain Dec's behavior from the first meeting with him aboard ship. The captain did not seem a bit worried about the possibility of Krayn attacking. That was strange, considering the Colicoids had accepted Jedi help.

Obi-Wan returned to the moment Krayn had first attacked the ship. There had been something in Anf Dec's manner that had bothered him then, too.

Obi-Wan focused on the memory, calling up details. He and Anakin had rushed to the bridge. The captain had given a flurry of orders. He had given every indication of being close to panic. Colicoids were unemotional beings. They were trained and held to a standard of reserve. Captain Anf Dec's obvious fear was an unusual display.

It wasn't his fear that troubled Obi-Wan, however. It was his outrage. That was what had flustered the captain — he had been caught by surprise. He seemed to take the attack personally.

But why? The Colicoids had enlisted the Jedi because they knew Krayn's attack was a possibility.

Or had they? Obi-Wan recalled that Chancellor Palpatine had been at the meeting. That was unusual. What it could indicate was that the Colicoids had been pressured to accept the Jedi. The Colicoids hadn't wanted them along not because they were wary of strangers, but because . . .

Because . . .

Why?

He didn't have the answer. But when he found it, Obi-Wan knew that it would lead him to his Padawan.

The Colicoid ship limped into one of the busy orbiting spaceports of Coruscant. Obi-Wan had already briefed Yoda and the Council by holographic transmission. He did not need to check in with the Temple. He took an air taxi to the Senate neighborhood below.

There, he hurried down the walkway opposite the grand Senate complex. He turned a corner and smiled when he saw a cheerful café painted blue with yellow shutters. The sign read DIDI AND ASTRI'S CAFÉ.

Didi and his daughter Astri had been good friends of Qui-Gon. Years ago Qui-Gon had volunteered to help Didi out of a "small difficulty" that had turned into a major mission involving the health and safety of an entire planet. Didi had survived a severe blaster wound and had gone on to become a successful café owner with his daughter. He no longer trafficked in stolen information, but he was still friends with the Jedi, and he kept his ears open.

Obi-Wan pushed open the door, remembering his first sight of the café thirteen years before. It had been cluttered, crowded, and dirty. Didi had reigned over the chaotic café with good cheer and a paternal way with his customers, but he'd never managed to keep the tables very clean or the food very nourishing. It was Astri who had transformed the café into a thriving restaurant with good food. Their clientele had slowly changed. Smugglers and criminals still ate here, but now they were joined by Senators and diplomats.

Obi-Wan stood for a moment, gazing over the heads of the customers to see if he could spot Didi or Astri. It had been nearly a year since he'd had the chance to visit them. They had both taken the news of Qui-Gon's death hard.

A tall woman a little older than Obi-Wan stood by a table, chatting with two customers who wore the robes of Senatorial aides. The woman's springy dark hair spilled out from underneath a white cap, and her white apron was stained with various colors. As she motioned to the aides, she nearly knocked over the teapot. Despite his anxiety, Obi-Wan grinned. Astri hadn't changed.

She looked up and her gaze met his. Astri's pretty face bloomed into a wide smile.

"Obi-Wan!" She rushed toward him, knocking over a chair in her haste to greet him. She threw herself into his arms. Obi-Wan hugged her, feeling her curls brush his cheeks. He had once felt awkward at such displays of emotion. Not anymore. Qui-Gon had taught him by example. Obi-Wan remembered how surprised he'd been as a Padawan to see Qui-Gon enthusiastically hug Didi.

She drew back. "Are you hungry? I have delicious stew today."

He shook his head. "I need help."

Her dancing eyes turned grave. "Let's find Didi."

A small, rotund man was already heading for them, his soft brown eyes widened in pleasure. He, too, enveloped Obi-Wan in a huge hug, though he barely reached Obi-Wan's shoulders. "How my eyes delight me!" he burbled. "The brave and wise Obi-Wan Kenobi, my good friend to whom I owe my life and my daughter!"

"Obi-Wan needs our help, Didi," Astri interrupted, for Didi would have gone on with flattery and sentiment.

Didi nodded. "Then come to the private office."

Obi-Wan followed Didi and Astri to a small, messy office behind the long counter. Although the café had improved significantly since Astri had taken over, the office was still a jumble of fading datasheets, mismatched plates, stacks of fresh tablecloths, and half-filled teacups.

"What can we do for you, my friend?" Didi asked. "Inadequate as I am, I am in your service."

"I'm searching for information only," Obi-Wan said. "Perhaps if you do not have answers, you could direct me to the party who does. I am investigating possible ties between a slave trader named Krayn and the Colicoids."

Didi frowned, and Astri wrinkled her nose.

"I don't like the Colicoid senators," she said. "Nothing is ever good enough for them."

"I have heard of Krayn," Didi said. "The galaxy would be well rid of such a fiend. I know of no connection, but . . ."

Obi-Wan waited. He knew that Didi was running over his vast list of contacts in his mind.

"Try Gogol at the Dor," Didi said at last. "I won't let him in this place since I found out what he traffics in. He did some work for Krayn, I heard."

"The Dor? I don't know it," Obi-Wan said.

"Of course you do," Astri said. "The Splendor. The readout letters kept getting shot off by stray blaster fire, so they finally gave up replacing them. Now everyone calls it the Dor." Astri shuddered. "Not that I'd set foot in the place."

Didi looked anxious. "You must be careful of your person, Obi-Wan. Gogol has mean bones."

He gave Obi-Wan a quick description, and Obi-Wan

was treated to two more fierce hugs from Didi and Astri. Promising to return for a meal, he hurried from the café.

He had been to the Splendor with Qui-Gon several times. He had come to know sections of the hidden city below the gleaming surface levels of Coruscant, where sunlight did not reach. Here, the walkways were narrow and littered, the twisting alleyways dangerous, and all of it barely lit by glow lamps that were constantly shot out and not replaced. Here was where one found the dregs of the galaxy, the worst criminals and lowlifes, where one could bargain cheaply for a death mark on an enemy's head.

The sleazy Splendor hadn't changed. The metal roof sagged, and the windows were ominously shuttered. The door was pockmarked with blaster fire. The letters D O R sputtered faintly in the dim light. Years ago as a Padawan, Obi-Wan had entered it nervous and unsure. Now he strode in as if he owned it.

It was not the same Imbat bartender at the bar, but it might well have been. He projected the same indifference to his customers, the same penchant for swatting his customers off their stools with a massive palm for trying too vigorously to signal for a refill.

Obi-Wan stood at the corner of the bar and waited.

He knew better than to signal for the Imbat's attention. Eventually the Imbat wandered over and bent his tall frame closer to hear Obi-Wan over the noise of the music and the whirl of the jubilee wheel.

"Gogol," Obi-Wan told him.

The Imbat signaled a table with his eyes. Obi-Wan slid a few credits across the bar.

Gogol was just as Didi had described him, a humanoid with a half-shaved head and long hair that straggled down his back. He played a dice game by himself, and bets were piled at both ends of his small table.

Obi-Wan sat across from him and said nothing.

Gogol did not look up from his game. "What do you want, chum?"

Obi-Wan slid a pack of credits across the table. "Information on Krayn."

Gogol eyed the packet without touching it.

"Then I'll need to see more than that."

Obi-Wan slid another packet of credits into the middle of the table. Gogol counted the two packets.

"I want to know what he's up to these days," Obi-Wan said.

"That's a tall order, chum." Gogol looked up. His beady eyes blinked rapidly. "Nobody knows the whole answer to that question."

"Give me part of it, then. Does he have any dealings with the Colicoids?"

"The table looks awfully empty," Gogol said.

Obi-Wan peeled off a few more credits.

Gogol licked his fingers in satisfaction as he counted the credits. Obi-Wan profoundly hoped that he was trustworthy, at least as far as information. Most types such as Gogol knew better than to lie. That would only get them in more trouble than they no doubt were in already.

"Word is that the Colicoids are taking over the spice trade," Gogol said. "They have secretly taken over the Kessel mines. Now they need a big processing planet. The last piece is the moon of Nar Shaddaa. The only way they can get it is to deal with Krayn. He controls the factories on Nar Shaddaa. He can't get enough spice from the caverns there, so he imports it from Kessel. It's a marriage made in paradise," Gogol cackled.

Obi-Wan knew Nar Shaddaa. Often called "smuggler's moon," it was a haven for criminals of all sorts. It was also an important link in the illegal spice trade. He had not known that Krayn was involved, however.

"Aga Culpa is the ruler of Nar Shaddaa. Doesn't he control the factories?" he asked.

"He might rule it, but he doesn't control it. Everyone on Nar Shaddaa answers to Krayn. So Krayn promises not to attack the Colicoid ships, and they promise to buy his slaves for the spice mines and use his factories. A good deal, eh, chum?"

A very good deal, Obi-Wan thought heavily, if one overlooked the fact that it involved cruelty, greed, and the selling of living beings for profit.

He stood and quickly exited the Dor. He paused outside for a moment. It had started to rain, and he welcomed the coolness on his cheeks.

The mention of the spice trade had immediately sparked a memory. He knew that Adi Gallia and Siri's last mission together had involved the smuggling activities on the Kessel Run. Spice was a legally controlled substance, but it also held enormous profits on the black market. The Jedi had been asked to try to break the back of the illegal trade once and for all. Adi Gallia and Siri had not been successful. Something had happened on the mission that had caused a deep rift between them.

Could this be connected to the Colicoids . . . and Krayn?

Obi-Wan began to walk in search of an air taxi. When he was unsure of which direction to go in next, his thoughts always returned to his Master. He remembered Qui-Gon's counsel, counsel Obi-Wan had passed on to Anakin about trusting his instincts and not allowing anger to cloud judgment. He should have listened to his heart.

Now his heart told him a simple truth. Siri would never betray the Jedi.

CHAPTER 12

Once again, Obi-Wan stood before the Jedi Council. It was just about the last place he wanted to be. He had lost his Padawan, who had been captured by a slave trader. The Colicoids were furious at the Jedi and had already raised objections in the Senate. He did not imagine that the Jedi Council was pleased with the outcome of his mission.

He wasted no time in trying to explain what had gone wrong. Jedi always focused on solutions.

"I have discovered that it is likely that the Colicoids are secretly in league with Krayn," Obi-Wan said immediately after greeting the Council members respectfully. "They wish to take over the spice trade, and Krayn wishes to be the sole supplier of slaves for the spice mines, both in the Kessel system and at Nar Shaddaa."

Some on the Council exchanged glances. If this were true, the illegal spice trade would thrive and grow.

"Bad news this is for the galaxy," Yoda remarked.

"We have reason to investigate what is happening on Nar Shaddaa, both to expose the Colicoids and bring down Krayn," Obi-Wan said. "And most important, I believe Anakin is on Nar Shaddaa. My guess is that the Colicoids were heading there after dropping us off at the original location."

"What is it you want of us, Obi-Wan?" Mace Windu asked, his dark eyes fixed on Obi-Wan's face.

"A very fast ship and permission to infiltrate Krayn's operation," Obi-Wan answered. "That is first of all. But second, and most important, I wish to be let in on a secret." He turned to Adi Gallia. "I believe that Siri has not turned to the dark side. I believe she is working undercover. If I infiltrate Krayn's operation, I need to know her mission."

Adi Gallia's regal face was impassive. Then she flicked a quick glance at Yoda and Mace Windu.

Slowly, Yoda nodded. "Correct you are, Obi-Wan."

"Siri is gathering information only," Adi Gallia said. "We discovered that the layers of power and control between Krayn and various governments are deep. We needed a full picture. Siri infiltrated the pirates and worked her way up to a position of trust. Krayn has no idea she is a Jedi. It is well known that he considers all Jedi his enemies and all his crew are ordered to execute any captured Jedi on the spot. It has taken Siri almost two years to gain this level of power in the Krayn organization. We cannot jeopardize her safety."

"But Anakin is with her —"

"Then she will protect him," Adi Gallia said firmly. "I am not sure if sending another Jedi is wise. It could compromise her identity."

"Perhaps," Mace Windu said. "But perhaps we have waited long enough. If the Colicoids are involved, that intensifies the pressure to bring about the collapse of the spice trade."

"I am worried about Anakin," Obi-Wan said. "There is only one way Siri can protect him. She must make him a slave. I do not know how he will react to that."

"Assume we do that he will act like a Jedi," Yoda said sharply, his gray-blue eyes blinking at Obi-Wan. "Patience he will find."

Obi-Wan could not argue without it reflecting badly on Anakin. But he knew that patience was not his Padawan's strong suit.

"Siri has sent us a coded message, Obi-Wan," Mace Windu said. "If you had not come to us, we would have sent for you. Anakin is safe. He is indeed a slave in a spice factory on Nar Shaddaa. She is keeping an eye on him."

"I must go there," Obi-Wan said.

"Patience you must have as well, Obi-Wan," Yoda said. "Confer with Adi Gallia we must."

"Please wait outside, Obi-Wan," Mace Windu said firmly.

Reluctantly, Obi-Wan left the room. He was too restless to sit in the waiting area outside the Council Room so he stood facing the door.

He had spoken bitterly to Siri aboard Krayn's ship. He regretted it now. He should have paid attention to what he had come to know about her over the years. He should have remembered how impressed he'd always been with her integrity and courage, her fierce commitment to the Jedi path. Instead he had spoken words of anger and betrayal.

And now Siri was the only thing standing between Anakin and survival.

He did not have long to wait. In just a few minutes, Adi Gallia slipped out of the Council Room.

"We have decided to grant your request. You can join Siri on Nar Shaddaa," Adi Gallia told him. He saw a rare crack in her regal bearing as she hesitantly put out a hand toward him, then withdrew it. "I know you will be careful, Obi-Wan, so I should not say it. But I must. Siri is in great danger. She has risked much. Please . . ."

Adi Gallia was a reserved and careful being. She did not ask for comfort and usually kept herself aloof. But Obi-Wan was moved by her distress and reacted spontaneously. He captured her hand and pressed it between his palms. "I will not fail you," he said.

CHAPTER 13

The siren blared, then clanged, announcing the start of another day. A day like yesterday. A day like tomorrow. If you survived it.

He had been here only five days, and it felt like a lifetime.

It could be far, far worse for us, Annie.

He understood Shmi's words now with every cell of his being. Compared to this, working for Watto on Tatooine had been a paradise.

The factories on Nar Shaddaa rose hundreds of stories and were spread out over hundreds of meters. The spice went through a multistep processing system. It could not be exposed to light, so the slaves lived in perpetual darkness. Much of the spice was off-loaded from ships that had made the Kessel Run. Other spice was cut in huge underground caverns. All of it was ferried up to the processing levels where the spice was dried or frozen, then processed into blocks.

Enormous power plants supplied energy for the endeavor. At the end of the long day, the workers filed out from the darkness, almost blinded, only to walk under a sky thick with toxic fumes. Taking a deep breath of the gray, particulate-laden air could lead to a long coughing fit.

Anakin already knew that the death rate among slaves was high. Children and the elders were especially vulnerable. From what he could see, many were dying by degrees.

Security was constant. The slaves were guarded by patrolling natives of Nar Shaddaa as well as droids. Escape was impossible. Even if one could manage to elude the guards and security devices, there would be nowhere to hide. The native citizens of Nar Shaddaa benefited from the slave trade. If they dissented, they were either threatened or bought off with huge bribes. The spaceports of this moon world were tightly controlled by Krayn. There was no way to break out and nowhere to go.

The whole operation ran incredibly smoothly, Anakin thought in disgust. Greed did not make Krayn sloppy.

Anakin had been assigned to gravsled duty. It was his job to transport the cut spice up to the processing levels. It was tedious, filthy work, much of it spent breathing in the dirt and dust from the caverns as he loaded the gravsled. Anakin was not aware of the fact that his job was considered lucky until he accidentally almost ran down a processing worker.

The slave, a female Twi'lek, had stepped back unexpectedly from her position at the loading dock, right into the path of his gravsled. Only Anakin's excellent reflexes prevented him from ramming her.

She whirled, her long head tails almost slapping Anakin in the face. "Watch where you're going, *schutta.*"

Anakin didn't know what a *schutta* was, but he knew when he was being insulted. "You're the one who stepped back," he pointed out. It was close to the end of a long day, and his mind and muscles were strained to the limit.

She advanced on him angrily, her blue skin flushed to a deeper hue. "Don't tangle with me, soft boy. Your privileges don't count around here."

"Quiet!" A slave on the assembly line warned them in a hiss. "Guard droid."

Anakin saw a droid with an electrojabber wheeling

down the aisle at a quick pace. A red beam shot out from the guard's chest and circled. This was how the droids kept track of each slave.

"It's looking for me," the Twi'lek said. "We can't leave the line, even for a moment." Her defiance was gone, and she sounded scared.

The slaves on the line immediately closed up so that the space where the Twi'lek had stood was gone. Anakin reached out and grabbed her arm. "Hop on."

She did as he said, and he reversed the gravsled and took off down another aisle.

"Crouch down underneath those bins," he murmured. "I'll look busy until it goes away."

"We all look alike to those droids," the Twi'lek muttered. "If I can slip back in place before it starts a head count, I might get away with this. Otherwise it's a prod or two with the electrojabber."

"Don't worry." Anakin gritted his teeth. On his first day, he had seen such an assault, on a slave too exhausted to work quickly. The guard droids were programmed to be especially vicious. They did not use "a prod or two," but employed the jabber until the victim was stunned into unconsciousness.

Anakin sped down the narrow lanes, occasionally stopping to unload a bin of spice so that he wouldn't look suspicious. He didn't want to leave the floor. The head count could begin at anytime, and he needed to be able to sneak the Twi'lek back in. Soon he would be in trouble himself. He was allowed a strict amount of time for his rounds.

He circled around the processing floor and returned to where he had a good vantage point. The guard droid was beginning a head count.

He heard a soft moan from behind him. "I'm dead."

"No, you're not." Anakin was not yet adept at moving objects with his mind. Yet he knew the Force was around him, even here. He drew it up from the scarred ground below, from the living energy of the beings around him, from the toxic sky. The Force bound all the slaves together, and they were part of one another and the rest of the galaxy, no matter how isolated they might feel. He struggled to block out everything but the pure quality of the Force. Slowly, he felt the Force grow around him, and he gathered it in and then sent it out to a pile of unprocessed spice sitting on the end of the worker line. One block of spice trembled, then another. Anakin held out a hand, feeling the Force move through him. The pile tumbled over, along with a stack of durasteel bins.

The guard droid immediately wheeled about. "Violation! Violation!"

"Go!" Anakin hissed.

The Twi'lek paused for one instant. Her eyes met his, and he saw a kind of forgiveness there. "My name is Mazie." Offering her name was a kind of apology, a gesture of friendship, he knew.

"Anakin."

She scooted out of the gravsled. The other slaves bunched up, shielding her for the few seconds it took her to slip back in line.

Anakin turned the gravsled. The guard droid could blame no one for the accident, since no one had been near. It circled, aiming its red laser light randomly, but the slaves continued to work. After a few seconds it went back to the head count. Mazie was safe.

Anakin was grateful for the hard physical training he'd been put through at the Temple. The slaves were rationed two scanty meals a day. He felt constant hunger like a beast inside him. He was not yet at Obi-Wan's level, capable of forgetting about food for long periods of time. He had to use meditation to allow his hunger to exist without weakening him.

As he parked his gravsled at the end of the day and headed for the lift tubes with the other slaves, he felt a deep weariness in his bones. He knew it had to do with a weariness of spirit as well.

Obi-Wan was looking for him. That he knew. He

was also confident that his Master would find him. But how long would it take? How much of him would be chipped away before it happened? Swallowing rage and fear did not fill up his empty belly, but it made him worry about losing his Jedi detachment.

He kept his eyes on the slave in front of him as they trudged to their quarters. A rain was falling, and it tasted bitter and metallic on Anakin's lips. He felt it soak his hair and unisuit.

Suddenly he felt a surge in the Force. Startled and hopeful, he lifted his head. Was his Master near? He searched the platforms high above. The factories and slave quarters were on the surface of Nar Shaddaa, but the city was built above. He did not see his Master. Instead, he saw Krayn.

The pirate stood on a platform a hundred meters high. Standing next to him was a nervous human man who Anakin did not know. Siri stood on Krayn's other side. Strange, but Siri's gaze seemed to focus right in on Anakin. He felt the Force gather, and he did not understand it. Did he have a connection to Siri? He didn't know. Was she demonstrating that she still could utilize her Jedi abilities? Maybe it was a warning. He didn't care.

He was about to drop his gaze when another being joined the others on the platform. Anakin was surprised to see the Colicoid captain, Anf Dec. What was he doing there? Weren't Krayn and the Colicoids bitter enemies? After all, Krayn had attacked Anf Dec's ship!

Krayn pointed below and made a sweeping gesture. Anf Dec nodded. Siri stared serenely ahead, no longer focused on Anakin.

He didn't know what it all meant. But somehow, he resolved to find out.

CHAPTER 14

Obi-Wan adjusted his blast pads and helmet. Then he checked to make sure his lightsaber was hidden among the jumble of weapons on his belt. He was disguised as a slave trader named Bakleeda, and he hoped he would pass. When he had gathered his concentration, he strode down the deserted corridor toward Security Room A.

It had taken careful planning to get him this far. He was on the space station Rorak 5, a half day's journey from Nar Shaddaa. It existed as a fuel stop for traveling freighters and was also well known for having a suite of security rooms available for meetings, clandestine or otherwise. The security rooms were outfitted with the highest defenses, and it was possible for all parties to leave their ships and travel there without being seen. As soon as Obi-Wan landed, a moving corridor attached to his landing ramp. He exited his ship and followed a set of verbal directions from overhead speakers to his destination.

Security Room A was where Krayn and the Colicoids were secretly meeting to discuss their takeover of the spice trade.

Every day it had taken to lay the groundwork for this meeting had cost him. His patience had been worn to shreds. Anakin had now been on Nar Shaddaa for two weeks. Enough time for him to be beaten. Imprisoned. Killed.

Obi-Wan did not dwell on it, but it was in his mind all the same. He knew that if he simply appeared on Nar Shaddaa as a Jedi he would risk Anakin's life as well as Siri's. The Council had warned him that his plan must be careful and perfect. He had given his word to Adi Gallia that this would be so.

Didi had helped him establish an identity as Bakleeda and introduced him to the right contacts. Didi had taken a great personal risk doing so, for Obi-Wan had told him that he would have to reveal himself as a Jedi eventually. He could not prevent that. It might become known that Didi had helped smuggle a Jedi into the Krayn organization. There were many in the criminal underworld who would not appreciate that. But

Didi had only swallowed twice rapidly and paled a bit before assuring Obi-Wan that he would take any risk for Obi-Wan and the memory of Qui-Gon.

Obi-Wan opened the door. The Colicoids were waiting, and he was relieved to see that he didn't know any of them. His face was hidden by his helmet, which came down over his eyes and nose, but it was better that no one could recognize him if something happened to dislodge it.

The three Colicoids gave him a brief glance but did not greet him. They stood at the round table, talking together in their own language. Words were interspersed with clicks and humming noises from their antennae and jointed legs. The Colicoids had been the ones who had put out word that they were looking for a slave trader with intelligence to represent them in a meeting. It had taken all of Obi-Wan's skill to convince their representative that he was the one they wanted.

One of the Colicoids turned to him. "I am Nor Fik. Do not speak unless asked a question."

Obi-Wan nodded.

They waited long minutes. Obi-Wan had been over the galaxy many times and had been present at scores of high-level meetings. On every world, no matter how different, one thing was always the same: The party with the most power was the last to arrive.

The door burst open and slammed against the wall. Krayn stood there, his bulk filling the doorway.

"My friends!"

The Colicoids nodded coolly at Krayn.

"An ion storm delayed me. A trifle." Krayn waved a hand. "I would travel through worse to get here."

The Colicoids pointedly ignored this obvious lie. Krayn strode into the room and a Wookiee with a scarred face and an eye patch crowded in. It was Krayn's associate, Rashtah. If Krayn meant to intimidate the Colicoids, it worked. The Wookiee was a fierce companion.

Krayn's sharp eyes traveled over Obi-Wan before returning to the Colicoids with a beam of friendship. "So this is your observer. Hardly necessary but I accept it as I do anything among friends. You see how conciliatory I am?"

"And we see that you have brought an observer as well," Nor Fik said, indicating Rashtah.

Krayn grinned as he sat, placing a long vibroblade on the table before him. "It was a long journey. I needed company."

Rashtah remained standing but let out a growl of amusement.

"This is a waste of time," Nor Fik snapped. "Let us get down to business."

Krayn's grin faded. "That is why I am here."

"We have control of the spice trade," Nor Fik said, seating himself opposite Krayn. The other two Colicoids seated themselves next to him. "We want you —"

Krayn held up a meaty hand. "Ah. Excuse me. I suggest that no lies be spoken here, in the interest of our continued good fellowship."

"Lies?" Nor Fik asked in disbelief.

Krayn leaned forward. "You do not control the spice trade. Not yet. You are still having trouble along the Kessel Run."

"That is because your pirates are still attacking our ships!" Nor Fik said angrily. "Despite your assurances to the contrary. And you yourself attacked our ship without warning when our highest level officer Anf Dec was aboard —"

"A regrettable mistake," Krayn said.

The Colicoid clicked its antennae together. "Now who is lying."

Krayn looked pained. "Trust. Trust — it's so necessary to have it between partners, Nor. I trust you. I see I have to work harder to make you trust me."

Obi-Wan was surprised at Krayn's methods. He had expected Krayn to be as much of a bully in the conference room as he was in the rest of the galaxy. Instead, he was holding back.

"Let's talk about Nar Shaddaa," Nor Fik said, not bothering to respond to Krayn. "You need more capital to keep those factories going. We will supply it. Once we have the entire spice trade firmly in our grasp, you will have the exclusive contract to process the spice in your Nar Shaddaa plants. It is in our best interest that you remain there as a cover, as we are members of the Senate now and should not be linked to a criminal organization. Naturally we will continue to support your slave raids."

Krayn smiled. "I admire your methods, Nor. I agree to step up attacks on other ships along the Kessel Run. That should allow you to close the noose on the trade there. I assume that the capital I need will be transferred into my accounts by this afternoon?"

"Perhaps. If we get some things clear."

For the first time, Krayn looked unnerved. He covered it with a smile. "Of course."

"My superiors demand an inspection of the factories on Nar Shaddaa," Nor Fik said. "After all, if we are giving you the contract, we have a right to a complete inspection. We are worried about your productivity — slaves have been dying in great numbers."

"It is unfortunate that lately there has been some increase in mortality . . ."

"Yes, it cuts into profits. It is harder and harder for you to conduct massive raids, thanks to the Senate cracking down on the slave trade," Nor Fik said. "If you don't keep your slaves healthy, you will have trouble replacing them."

"A healthy slave is a slave who dreams of escape," Krayn said.

"That is what security is for," Nor Fik said. "I am not suggesting that you pamper them. Feed them enough to keep going. When your ship is struggling, you must conserve your fuel, but reach your destination."

Obi-Wan felt revulsion rise deep within him. Krayn and Nor Fik were talking about living beings as if they were machines to be maintained.

You're the one who doesn't understand!

Anakin's tortured words filled his brain. His Padawan had been right. He hadn't understood. He couldn't understand the depths of Anakin's feeling. As a child, Anakin had lived every day with the knowledge that his life meant nothing. That he was a possession, not a living being.

Obi-Wan struggled to maintain his calm. His heart

cried out to move, to get on a ship and go to Nar Shaddaa.

"There is nothing wrong with the treatment of slaves on Nar Shaddaa," Krayn said, anger beginning to color his voice. "I know best —"

"Perhaps. But we need to see the operation first-hand."

"Captain Anf Dec has been given a tour."

"And he has recommended an independent observer. He was not allowed the access he expected."

Krayn looked astonished. "He didn't say a word! Naturally we would have given him a tour of any part of the operation —"

"He was put off with excuses and promises," Nor Fik interrupted. "And he is not experienced in the slave trade. Neither are we, nor are we qualified to judge the work ability of such an assortment of beings. Therefore we have found an independent observer to report back to us. This is Bakleeda. He is in your business, and is willing to act as consultant for us."

Obi-Wan took one step forward.

"He will travel to Nar Shaddaa and you will give him free and open access. This is not negotiable. Agreed?"

Krayn hesitated. Obi-Wan could see a deep red flush on his neck. It was the only sign of his rage.

"Agreed."

Obi-Wan remained impassive, but excitement flared within him. He had free access to Nar Shaddaa.

CHAPTER 15

Anakin was so exhausted that he craved his sleep-mat, on the hard ground in the large durasteel ware-house that served as slave quarters. The slaves were packed tightly in rows, and the rain came through leaks in the roof that made puddles that never dried. Sleep-mats were thin and tattered, and the cold and damp seeped up from the ground to chill bodies that had already been pushed to their limits.

No matter how much he craved sleep, it was elu-sive. Anakin lay awake long after others around him were breathing quietly, huddled under thin blankets, some pressed close to one another for warmth. He stared up at a tiny sliver of sky he could glimpse through the roof. He could not see a star, but he imag-ined one. He imagined his Master in a ship speeding past that star, straight to Nar Shaddaa.

Movement close to him jolted him to his elbows.

Anakin peered through the darkness, expecting one of the scavenging creatures that overran the slave quarters. Instead, he saw someone crawling toward him. It was Mazie.

She squeezed in between him and his neighbor, who obligingly grunted and rolled slightly away to make room.

"I just wanted to thank you for today," she whispered. "I wasn't very nice to you at the beginning."

"I know," Anakin said with his characteristic bluntness. "I've been thinking about that. Why did you call me a *schutta*? What does it mean?"

Mazie squirmed. "I spoke harshly. A *schutta* is a weasel creature in my language. You see, you were assigned gravsled duty. It's easy duty, reserved for informants and favorites of the Nar Shaddaa guards. You must have someone protecting you."

"But I don't," Anakin protested. "I've only just arrived." But suddenly he knew who his protector was: Siri. But why should she protect him? Surely she'd lost any sense of loyalty to the Jedi long ago. He would never forget the bitterness in his Master's voice. Obi-Wan just wasn't wrong about people.

She must be playing with him, keeping him protected so that other slaves would despise him. Eventually, she would betray him.

Mazie shrugged. "If you have protection, I guess I shouldn't say anything. My daughter was favored by Krayn, though she'd done nothing to earn it. Berri is a domestic worker-slave in Krayn's kitchen. Every day I thank my stars that it is so. At least she is not working here. The Nar Shaddaa guards aren't bad, but the droids kill without mercy."

"Why do the people of Nar Shaddaa work as guards?" Anakin wondered.

"The planet's leader, Aga Culpa, has made an agreement with Krayn that its people will remain free in exchange for Krayn's control of the factories," Mazie explained. "There is not much honest work on Nar Shaddaa, and the guards are well paid. So tell me, how do you come to be here? Is this your first experience as a slave?"

"I was free when I was captured, but I was raised as a slave on Tatooine," Anakin said.

"Tatooine! But that is where Berri and I lived! We were colonists. My husband and I started a moisture farm. Berri and I were taken in a raid. It was ironic — there were many raids on Ryloth. We left our home planet to escape them when Berri was born. She is now sixteen."

"How long ago were you captured?" Anakin asked eagerly.

"Ten years now," Mazie said. "I used to dream of escape. No more. My husband was killed in the raid along with countless others. He resisted."

"Did you happen to know a human woman named Hala?" Anakin asked eagerly. Perhaps Hala was still alive!

"Yes, we arrived here together. They brought us to processing. Hala saw Krayn and suddenly broke out of the line. She tried to kill him." Mazie cast her clear gaze down. "He struck her down and then . . . he made an example of her."

Anakin shuddered. He did not want to know the details.

"And he took her necklace as a souvenir," he muttered.

"Yes. I used to make many friends among the slaves," Mazie said. "No more. Too many die. There is no escape, Anakin, so do not imagine that there could be one for you. Krayn has a death grip on us. He will never let go."

The anger that always lay in wait deep within him surged. He directed it at Krayn. If it was the last act of his life, he would kill that fiend.

No. It is not the Jedi way. Your anger feels like revenge.

He was trembling with rage. He knew suddenly

that he could not wait for Obi-Wan to rescue him. If he didn't try to escape, something essential in him would die.

Krayn would win. He saw the battle clearly and personally. It was him or Krayn.

"Do not fear, Anakin," Mazie said, misunderstanding his distress. "A slave's life is short. It will soon be over."

"No," Anakin said. "I will find a way out."

CHAPTER 16

Obi-Wan was given permission to land at Krayn's personal platform.

"You see?" Krayn had boasted back on Rorak 5. "I am showing every consideration."

Privately, Obi-Wan thought that someone who was doing the right thing for good motives did not call attention to it, but he did not point this out to the Colicoids. He had a feeling that Nor Fik felt the same.

He accessed the hatch and exited his transport. He was surprised there was no one to meet him. Technically he was allowed unlimited access, but Obi-Wan had felt sure that Krayn would try to control his movements. Perhaps they were keeping him under surveillance.

There was no time to waste. Obi-Wan was anxious to get to the factories. Since it was also the objective of his alias Bakleeda, he would attract no suspicion by heading there immediately.

It wasn't hard to spot the factories below. Black smoke belched from the stacks and then passed through scrubbers. The air up in the city was clean, but Obi-Wan looked down on thick toxic air below.

Obi-Wan accessed the turbolift to take him to the moon's floor. He stepped inside and felt the turbolift drop. Soon he would find Anakin. His entire being was focused on that.

Suddenly, the turbolift stopped. Obi-Wan felt a surge in the Force that warned him of danger a split second before the trapdoor overhead opened and Rashtah dropped down.

The turbolift shook with the impact of the Wookiee hitting the floor. As he landed, he struck out with one mighty hand. The blow sent Obi-Wan flying against the wall of the turbolift. His head hit the durasteel with a crack.

He reached for his lightsaber as Rashtah bellowed and came at him, casually smashing him again with a fist like a cannon. Obi-Wan felt the blow through his body armor. His arm went numb. He knew that when it came to brute strength, he was no match for a Wookiee. The last thing he could wish was to be trapped in a turbolift with one.

He reached with his other hand for his lightsaber. At the same time he whirled to evade Rashtah in a spinning motion. There was not much room to maneuver. The Wookiee definitely held the advantage. As Obi-Wan spun by him, Rashtah reached out and hit him again, this time with an elbow slamming into his stomach.

The air left Obi-Wan's lungs in a whoosh. Rashtah followed the blow with one to his chin, and he fell to his knees. He had not yet been able to get his lightsaber out of his belt. The blows were coming too fast, and now he only had the use of one hand. He had tucked his lightsaber securely inside the belt in order to conceal it. That had been a mistake.

Things didn't look good.

The smell of the creature's wet fur made it even harder to breathe. Obi-Wan scrambled between Rashtah's legs to come up on his other side. He struck out with a series of fast combinations, using his legs as weapons. Rashtah grunted and tried to capture one leg, but Obi-Wan was too fast. At last he was able to activate his lightsaber.

Rashtah let out a surprised bellow that shook the walls of the turbolift. Obi-Wan attacked, whirling and diving, as Rashtah tried to defend himself. He gave up on his fists and withdrew an electrojabber and a vibro-ax. Obi-Wan guessed his objective. With the electro-jabber he would paralyze Obi-Wan and then administer the death blow with the vibro-ax.

It was imperative to avoid the electrojabber. If he was hit, he could be paralyzed for an hour, at least. Already feeling was coming back to his numb arm. Obi-Wan focused on healing it. It could mean the difference in the battle, for the Wookiee thought his right arm was useless.

Obi-Wan struck at Rashtah, but the creature deflected the blow with the vibro-ax. The two weapons tangled and smoke filled the air.

Turning, Obi-Wan suddenly tossed the lightsaber from his left hand to his right. He leaped forward and came at the Wookiee with a sky-to-ground sweep. He slashed at the creature's chest.

Rashtah's eyes glazed, and his howl was terrible. He dropped the electrojabber and clutched at his wound. At the same time he swung the vibro-ax. Obi-Wan brought the lightsaber down on the Wookiee's arm. The creature fell over, his mournful death cry fading as his spirit left his body.

Obi-Wan collapsed against the wall. Sweat stung his eyes. Rashtah had tried to kill him, but he did not glory in this outcome. Death at such close quarters was a devastating thing.

He hit the turbolift button and the lift dropped. By the time it reached the planet floor, Obi-Wan had risen, adjusted his body armor and helmet, and tucked his lightsaber back in his belt.

The doors opened. He was in a small enclosed anteroom. Through a window he could see a deserted yard outside. It held factory equipment that rusted in the rain.

He had a problem. If Rashtah's body was found, suspicion would be on him. Krayn wanted it that way. The pirate was clever. If Rashtah had succeeded in killing him, fine. But if the slave trader Bakleeda somehow managed to kill the Wookiee, then Krayn could demand his removal from the planet, or kill Bakleeda himself. Either way, he would be rid of interference.

Obi-Wan dragged the heavy body of the Wookiee out into the drizzle. He rolled it underneath a pile of outdated machines.

Soon Krayn would look for Rashtah. The Wookiee would be found. Obi-Wan had less time than he'd thought. He had to find Anakin.

CHAPTER 17

As Anakin steered the gravsled to the drop-off pile, Mazie stepped closer. She had changed places with the worker closest to the pile, and she and Anakin exchanged smiles and glances throughout the day. It made the work almost bearable, Anakin thought.

He made note of the fact that although Mazie had claimed not to make friends anymore, she had certainly befriended him. He noticed that she watched out for others, too. If a worker's output was slackening, she quickly organized other slaves to help. If they spread the work among themselves, the droids didn't notice. As she passed down the line, she often put a hand on a shoulder here, or bestowed a quick smile there.

She had the loyalty of the slaves. Anakin both admired that and filed the information away.

Mazie drifted closer as he unloaded the battered durasteel bins full of cut spice.

"I have a little bread. Berri brought it to me," she whispered. "Here."

She pressed a bit of bread in his hand.

"No," Anakin said, trying to give it back.

"You're young. You need your energy." Mazie quickly drifted back. If he followed her, he might attract the attention of the patrolling droids, and she knew it.

Anakin pocketed the piece of bread and finished unloading the bins. He would distribute it to a worker below who he noticed had been weakening daily.

He climbed up on the gravsled and hit the forward controls, ready to take the long tunnel down to the caverns below.

Suddenly Siri stood in front of him, her hands on her hips. He jerked the gravsled to a stop.

"What is in your pocket?" she asked.

He did not answer.

Her lips thinned. "Come with me, slave."

Anakin climbed off the gravsled. Siri led him to a corner away from the patrolling droids, the hooded gazes of the slaves, and noise of the machines.

She turned on him immediately, her blue eyes snapping. "It is foolish to break the rules here. You are not supposed to fraternize with other slaves during work hours. No speaking is allowed unless a few words are needed for work."

Anger sputtered through a weary Anakin. "You do not have to repeat the rules to me."

"So you choose to break them? That is stupid. You will call attention to yourself, and attention is never good here. Your duty is to keep your eyes down and survive."

"I am a slave, Siri," Anakin said, not bothering to hide the contempt in his voice. "I am your prisoner. Isn't that enough for you? Don't pull me aside to rub my face in it. How dare you?"

Siri looked at him, shocked.

"Who are you to tell me my duty?" Anakin spat out. "You betrayed us all. You turned your back on the Jedi and embraced the dark side. Now you are Krayn's spy. The ally of a slave trader, the most contemptible, despicable being in the galaxy —"

A low chuckle reached his ears. Anakin sputtered to a stop as Krayn stepped around the corner.

"Such praise," he said mockingly. "How lucky I am to be such an icon of evil to my property. It means I am doing something right."

"I was just reprimanding this slave," Siri said. "He is new and did not know the rules."

Krayn turned to her and his expression was no longer amused. "So you are a Jedi. What did he call you? Siri?"

"No longer," Siri said. "I left them long ago, but they have this ridiculous code of loyalty. They think they own me. No one owns me!"

"Ah, you forget something," Krayn said. "I do."

Siri's eyes blazed. "*No one* owns me, Krayn."

Suddenly guard droids appeared around the corner and surrounded them.

"I left the Jedi for good," Siri said. There was no trace of begging in her voice. "I have been your loyal associate, Krayn."

"Yes, the best I ever had," Krayn said sadly. "Yet I cannot take the chance that you are a spy. Whether you are loyal or not doesn't matter — you are a risk. You were the one to advise me about taking unnecessary risks, Zora. Isn't it ironic that you will be put to death because of that?"

He turned to the droids. "These two are Jedi. Take them into the security prison to await execution." He smiled at Siri. "I think a little show for the Colicoids might be a good start for our partnership."

The guards surrounded Anakin and Siri in a tight circle. They marched the two prisoners down the row toward the exit. Mazie looked at him furtively and tried to give him a smile of support. He gave her a meaningful glance.

The guards marched Anakin and Siri to Krayn's

complex high above the factory floor. Anakin was surprised that Siri did not try to resist. He wondered if
she still had her lightsaber somewhere. If she had,
surely she would use it.

They were locked together in the lowest level of
Krayn's complex in a high-security cell. Anakin put his
palms on the door as if he could force it open.

"The Colicoids are already here for the meeting,"
Siri said. "It might not be too long."

Anakin didn't speak to her.

The guards had stripped Siri of her weapons, but
she reached into a slit in her utility belt and came up
with a small device. She activated it.

"No listening devices," she murmured. "Good."

Anakin said nothing. If she thought he was going
to speak to a traitor, she was crazy as well as evil.

"Anakin," Siri said quietly, "I am still a Jedi. I am
working undercover."

He turned, surprised. "How do I know you're telling
the truth?"

"You don't. You have to trust me. Even Obi-Wan
didn't know. No one at the Temple does, except for
the Jedi Council. This was our final attempt to clean
up Nar Shaddaa and end Krayn's reign of terror."

Anakin waited as Siri's words sunk in. His brain did

not weigh her words. He allowed himself to feel them, to tap into Siri's essence.

"I believe you," he said at last.

"Good." She sat cross-legged on the floor. "Not that my being a Jedi helps us at the moment. But it makes things a little more pleasant in here."

Anakin was suddenly stabbed with guilt. "I blew your cover!"

She waved a hand. "It's all right."

"It's not! I compromised the mission. Obi-Wan has always instructed me to be careful with what I say in anger."

"I am sure that he also told you that I am responsible for my own risks," Siri said firmly. "And I'm sure he advised you to recognize the danger of your impulsiveness and then move on without blame, only wisdom."

Anakin smiled. "You sound just like him."

"I know him well. He has this habit of telling you the truth just when you don't want to hear it."

Anakin laughed and discovered that he liked Siri. He sat down opposite her.

"I've been keeping an eye on you, Anakin," she said. "I'm impressed with your kindness and bravery. I saw how you tried to help the weak ones when you could."

Anakin's grin faded. "I know what it's like to be a slave."

"Yes. And it is unfortunate that events placed you here. You have shown remarkable patience and strong will. I believe you'll make a fine Jedi."

"If I'm not executed first."

"It's not over yet," Siri said. "Obi-Wan is somewhere on Nar Shaddaa, I'm sure. The Council sent him here."

Anakin brightened. "He is? But how can he get to us?"

"He'll find a way."

"So Krayn is in league with the Colicoids," Anakin said. "That's why Captain Dec was here."

"The Colicoids are taking over the spice trade, and they need to make a deal with Krayn to process the spice here on Nar Shaddaa. The leader of Nar Shaddaa will look the other way, as he always does."

Anakin nodded thoughtfully. What Siri had just told him reinforced his own suspicions as well as the forming of his plan.

"We can't afford to wait here for rescue," Anakin told Siri. "If the Colicoids are here on Nar Shaddaa, we have to act now."

"And do what?"

"If we can convince the Colicoids that it is in their best interests to take over the Nar Shaddaa operation, then Nar Shaddaa will come under the laws of the Republic, since the Colicoids are members."

"True," Siri admitted.

"So slavery will be outlawed."

"That's exactly why they wouldn't do it," Siri said. "They need slaves. Or rather, they convince themselves they do out of their own greed."

"Exactly. So we have to use their greed against them. We have to convince the Colicoids that they can still make enormous profits without slaves. They can do this by eliminating Krayn as the middleman. They won't have to give him a cut of the profits, or rely on his abilities to run the factories, or worry about him cheating them."

"What makes you think the Colicoids would listen to that argument?" Siri asked. "They're very cautious."

"Their caution and their greed will force them to listen," Anakin said. "But we have to make them think that if they don't do it, they will lose everything. I'll bet they already distrust Krayn."

"Everybody does," Siri said. "That is, if they're smart."

"If we can convince the Colicoids that Krayn has a

shaky hold on Nar Shaddaa and is in danger of losing the factories, they'll be more willing to take the chance to overthrow him."

"Why would they think that?" Siri asked.

"Because there will be a slave rebellion while the Colicoids are here," Anakin responded quickly. "The slaves will blow up part of the factory. If the Colicoids see this, they might seize that moment of weakness to take over."

Siri stared at him. "But why would the slaves rebel?"

"Because they want to be free," Anakin said.

Siri shook her head. "It's not that simple, Anakin. The guards hold those slaves in the grip of fear. Their brutality over the years has been great. The slaves risk too much."

"If they felt that they had a chance . . ." Anakin said thoughtfully.

"Yes, some sort of guarantee that made it worth the risk," Siri said slowly. "I have an idea. You're leaving out the third party in all this — the leader of Nar Shaddaa. He is in control of the civilian guards. If we can convince him that it's in his best interests to back the Colicoids over Krayn, he can instruct the guards to look the other way when the slaves rebel. Nar Shaddaa will become part of the Republic, and the natives will enjoy the benefits of alliances and trade."

"Of course!" Anakin enthused. "That's the missing key."

"I've been involved in some high-level meetings," Siri told him. "The Colicoid representatives know me. If I can get to them, I can lay the whole thing out. I can make them suspicious of Krayn's abilities. They'll trust me, since I'm his advisor. I know Aga Culpa, the leader of Nar Shaddaa, too."

"And I'll talk to the slaves," Anakin said.

Siri sighed. "There's only one problem. We're in a high-security cell. And both our lightsabers are in my quarters. We can't break out."

Anakin smiled.

She raised an eyebrow at him. "Don't tell me you have a plan for that, too."

"Of course," Anakin said.

Siri shook her head. "You remind me of someone I knew well years ago. He never let up, either. Made me think fast to keep up with him." She grinned. "Just don't ever tell Obi-Wan I said so."

"It's funny," Anakin said. "I thought you hated him."

Siri stretched her muscles. "Of course I don't hate him. He just gets on my nerves." Her vivid blue eyes glinted. "But then again, most beings do."

CHAPTER 18

Obi-Wan had tried everything he knew. He had reached out with the Force, trying to locate Siri or Anakin. His Padawan's connection was so strong that he'd felt sure that once he was inside the factory he would be able to locate him. But all he felt was a void.

He had walked over much of the factory, and the day was waning. He had looked into the faces of hundreds of slaves. He had seen misery and sickness and exhaustion. He had not seen his Padawan.

He found a private place to contact the Temple. Adi Gallia answered his call.

"We have lost contact with Siri," she said. "We cannot help you, Obi-Wan. You're on your own."

He acknowledged the transmission and quickly tucked the comlink in his tunic. Something indeed was very wrong. It was time to locate Krayn.

Obi-Wan took the lift tube to Krayn's sprawling complex. As he walked toward Krayn's private quarters, he felt a disturbance in the Force. He paused, but he couldn't trace it. Still, it worried him.

Krayn's receiving room surprised Obi-Wan. He had expected richness, a display of Krayn's enormous wealth to show how important he was. But the room was almost bare. The floor was of plain rough stone. The only sign of Krayn's ego was an enormous chair carved out of rare greel wood.

Krayn was standing as Obi-Wan arrived. "So," he said in a jovial tone, "have you seen all that you have come to see?"

"No," Obi-Wan reported shortly. "I have toured some of the factory on my own, but I request a guide. Someone who knows your operation well."

"Hmmm," Krayn said. "That would be Rashtah. Strange, however. No one has been able to find him today. You didn't happen to run into him in your travels, did you? A large Wookiee with a bad temper?"

It was a test, of course. Krayn was playing with him. He knew very well that if Obi-Wan was now standing in front of him, the Wookiee had failed.

"No. Perhaps someone else can substitute."

"I will find someone, of course. I'll send them to you."

"I'll be on the factory floor —"

Krayn's eyes glittered. "Don't worry. I always know where to find you."

Obi-Wan's sense of unease was growing. Krayn felt too secure. Why? Did he know that Obi-Wan was a Jedi? Or was he confident because his deal with the Colicoids was close to being completed?

Obi-Wan paused at the same spot he had felt a disturbance in the Force earlier. He reached out, gathering the Force around him, pushing himself to reach deeper, farther, wider.

He did not feel an answering call from Anakin. Yet he knew one thing: His greatest fear had not been realized. His Padawan was still alive.

But if he was alive, that meant he was thinking. Planning. Obi-Wan fervently hoped his impulsive Padawan would remember patience and caution. At least he could be with Siri . . .

Apprehension suddenly snaked through Obi-Wan. If Anakin and Siri were together, anything could happen.

Hours later, a tiny slit in the door opened and a tray was pushed through. On it was a protein wafer as hard as a rock, some water, and a moldy piece of bread.

"No, thank you," Siri said.

Anakin approached the tray eagerly. He tore open

the piece of bread. Inside was a message written on a scrap of durasheet.

WHAT CAN I DO?   BERRI

Siri looked over his shoulder. "Who is that?"

"She's my friend Mazie's daughter. She works in the kitchens here." Anakin was glad Mazie had thought of asking for Berri's help. He had counted on it. "Where did you hide your lightsaber? And, while you're at it, mine?"

"In my quarters," Siri answered. "Underneath my sleep-couch."

"That's original."

Siri looked annoyed. "It's handy. And no one ever cleans. I didn't have to worry about being discovered. There are weapons checks throughout Krayn's complex. I couldn't take a chance that my lightsaber would be found."

Anakin wrote carefully with the implement wrapped in the durasheet.

ZORA'S BED.   WEAPONS.

He placed the tray back on the shelf. Minutes later, the slit opened. The tray was grabbed from outside.

"This could be a trick," Siri said worriedly.

"If it is, we're no worse off," Anakin pointed out. "And it's not a trick. Mazie is loyal."

After a moment, Siri nodded. "I trust who you trust."

They sat down to wait. The minutes ticked by, then an hour.

"I was never good at the patience exercises at the Temple," Siri groaned.

"Me, neither," Anakin admitted.

Siri blew out a breath. "Obi-Wan always was."

At last the panel slid open, and two lightsabers tumbled to the floor, followed by two comlinks.

"Thank you, Berri," Anakin whispered through the opening. He could not see Mazie's daughter. "Now get back to your post."

They waited until they were sure that Berri was clear. Then they activated their lightsabers. Anakin felt a surge of confidence as he saw the blue glow. He didn't feel like a slave anymore. He was a Jedi again.

Together they cut through the thick door. The durasteel peeled back, and Siri stepped through the opening, followed by Anakin.

There were no guards in the corridor.

"Krayn always trusts high-tech security too much," Siri muttered. "Let's head for Aga Culpa."

There were only three droid guards stationed in

the entrance to the basement prison. Siri and Anakin paused after peeking around the corner to glimpse them.

"We don't have time for complicated strategy," Siri said. "Let's just charge them."

They activated their lightsabers again and were on the droids before they could respond to the attack. They both leaped high in the air and then came down, slicing their lightsabers through the droids and splitting them in half. As the third droid kept up blaster fire, it retreated to the console desk, no doubt to raise an alarm. Anakin cut down the droid while Siri whirled and buried her shaft in the console communication panel. It sizzled and smoked.

"We'd better hurry now," Siri said.

She led the way to an exit following a little-used passageway. "This is Krayn's private escape route," she told Anakin. "It leads to his landing platform, and it's only a short distance from there to Aga Culpa. Krayn insisted that Culpa enjoy the comfort of the complex, but actually he just wanted to keep an eye on him."

Anakin followed Siri to Krayn's landing platform and then to another walkway that led to another quadrant of the complex. Siri accessed the door and walked in.

They found Aga Culpa sitting in front of a holographic game.

"Busy as usual, I see," Siri said, striding in and shutting off the game.

Aga Culpa looked up. The expression on his face was such an odd mixture of outrage, embarrassment, and apprehension that Anakin was almost tempted to laugh. Culpa was a thin humanoid male with a slack-muscled body that he clothed in skintight tech fabric. He wore a tiny matching cap on his bald head.

"How dare you burst into my private quarters!" he blustered. Then he looked nervous. "Does Krayn want to see me?"

"No. I do." Siri sat astride a chair. "This is my slave, Anakin. We may speak freely in front of him."

Anakin bristled inside at being called a slave, but he understood the necessity for it.

"I've come to give you a message from the Colicoids," Siri said. "They are going to take over the factories of Nar Shaddaa. Naturally Krayn is not aware of this."

The apprehension on Aga Culpa's face changed to fear. "Take over?" he whispered.

"They have the power," Siri said. "And a close associate of Krayn's has agreed to help them. That's me. I always liked you, Culpa, so I'm giving you the opportunity to join us."

"Against Krayn?" Aga Culpa gripped the arms of his chair.

"It would be a smart move. And easy. All you have to do is nothing. Tell the guards of the Nar Shaddaa factories not to interfere with the slaves."

"I can't do that," Aga Culpa said. "Krayn would kill me."

"Are you so sure that you're safe from the Colicoids if you do not?" Siri asked pleasantly.

Aga Culpa's look of fearful unease intensified. He shook his head. "N-no. I can't go against Krayn."

Siri gave a quick look of exasperation at Anakin. Obviously Aga Culpa was too weak and paralyzed with terror to take a risk. She shrugged. Anakin knew what was in her mind.

He felt the Force gather in the room. It was powerful, and he admired Siri's grasp of it. She turned her attention back to Aga Culpa and passed a hand in front of his face.

"Contact the Nar Shaddaa slave guards. If there is a revolt, order them to do nothing."

"I will order them to do nothing. I will contact the guards." Aga Culpa's voice was toneless, but the mind suggestion had worked. On such a weak will as Culpa's, it had been easy.

"Do it now."

They watched as Aga Culpa activated his comlink and spoke to the commanding officer. He overrode the officer's expression of disbelief with a firm repeat of the order.

"Do it or suffer the consequences," Siri whispered.

"Do it or suffer the consequences," Aga Culpa repeated. He shut off the communication.

"Thanks, Culpa. I appreciate your support." Siri sprang off the chair athletically and strode toward the door.

As soon as she and Anakin were outside, she frowned. "The Colicoids won't be so easy. Jedi mind tricks won't work. I'll have to go alone, Anakin."

"I need to talk to the slaves, anyway."

"I don't need to wish you luck," Siri said. "I know you can do it."

"Luck always helps. I'll wait for your signal."

Anakin ran toward the turbolift. He had gained great confidence in Siri.

It took Anakin a few minutes of careful strategy to get around the patrolling guard droids in the factory. He stealthfully slipped next to Mazie on the assembly line, hoping the guards would not do a sudden head count.

Quickly, he explained the situation and what he needed.

She gazed at him, amazed. "You really do mean to break out, don't you."

"Not alone," Anakin said. "With all of us, together."

"I can't do it, Anakin," Mazie said in a low tone as her fingers continued to work. "I can't ask them to risk so much."

"All we have to worry about is the droids. The Nar Shaddaa guards will look the other way."

"The droids are enough."

"What if I created a diversion? An explosion? I know where the explosives are kept in the caverns."

Mazie bit her lip. "I don't know . . ." she murmured.

"It's the only way, Mazie. Do you want to end your life here, like this? Do you want Berri to live as a slave?"

"You're not fair."

"But I'm right."

"Perhaps . . . perhaps there is a core group who will revolt," she said slowly.

"You will contact them?"

She nodded.

"Others will see us succeed and will join us," Anakin said confidently.

"I hope you are right," Mazie murmured. Her hands now trembled as she worked.

Anakin slipped away. The end of the shift was only minutes away. Everything depended on Siri now.

CHAPTER 19

Unable to find Anakin or Siri, Obi-Wan had to report to the Colicoid delegation or risk blowing his cover. He was just beginning his report when Siri burst in.

Relief flooded Obi-Wan as he saw she was safe. He stepped back against the wall so that she would not be distracted if she recognized him. He saw determination on her face — Siri had a plan.

"You must excuse me for coming uninvited to this meeting," she said, turning to Nor Fik. "I come to you without Krayn's knowledge."

Nor Fik looked surprised but immediately tried to hide it. "Go on."

"It is my belief that if you allow Krayn to keep control of the spice factories on Nar Shaddaa, you will lose them and we will all lose the enormous profits we gain from them," Siri said.

"And why should we listen to you?" Nor Fik asked in a frosty tone.

"Because I know more about Krayn's operations than he does," Siri said. "The slaves are poised to revolt. He doesn't have enough security to handle it."

Nor Fik turned to Obi-Wan. "And what do you think, Bakleeda?"

"What I've seen supports what she says," Obi-Wan said shortly. He knew that if he said too much it could backfire.

Siri looked at him curiously. She knew something was off, but she hadn't recognized him. Obi-Wan was tempted to reach out through the Force, but resisted. She didn't need to know who he was. He had guessed her plan and would follow her lead.

Siri's fingers hooked into her utility belt as she waited for Nor Fik to make a decision. Obi-Wan saw her finger tense, then relax. He glimpsed a signaling device tucked inside.

She was sending a signal. That could only mean one thing. Anakin.

"This needs further study," Nor Fik said. "We cannot make a decision based on a few opinions. We are not prepared to take over the entire operation of Nar Shaddaa."

"But you expect to someday," Siri guessed shrewdly. "You won't cut Krayn in forever. You will observe his methods and how you can improve them, and you will move in. He will be no match for you. It is my belief that the spice factories can be run more efficiently with workers rather than slaves. The help you would receive from the Republic would be of enormous benefit. You already have great power in the Senate."

"You speak eloquently, Zora, but again, I must —"

Nor Fik's words were drowned out by a sudden explosion. Siri was almost thrown to the floor, but kept her feet. One of the Colicoids tumbled off his chair and quickly righted himself, embarrassed.

Siri, Obi-Wan, and Nor Fik hurried to the window. They had a panoramic view of the spice processing plant below. A large column of smoke was snaking up from one of the buildings.

"The rebellion has begun," Siri said. "Do you believe me now?"

Nor Fik stared down at the factory. A moment later, the doors opened and slaves spilled out. Some of them carried weapons they had stolen from the Nar Shaddaa guards.

"Where is Krayn?" Nor Fik asked Siri.

"In his quarters."

"Perhaps it is time he was . . . detained."

Siri put a hand on the hilt of her lightsaber. "I can arrange that."

CHAPTER 20

Anakin had gathered the team of slaves to set the explosives. He had destroyed a small squad of guard droids with a combination of the Force and his lightsaber. The victory over the guard droids had caused a giant cheer to rise among the slaves, and soon they stripped the droids of weapons and fashioned their own. The rebellion spread.

Anakin stopped only long enough to ensure that the explosion had worked and that the slaves had the upper hand in the battle. The Nar Shaddaa guards all quickly put down their blasters and left the area. The slaves picked up the weapons and turned on the droids.

Anakin raced from the factory toward the turbolift. If he knew Krayn, he guessed that the pirate would not remain on Nar Shaddaa. As soon as Krayn knew the rebellion could not be put down, he would head for his transport. Anakin intended to stop him.

He burst out on the landing platform in time to see Krayn hurrying toward his ship. The pirate carried a blaster in one hand and a vibro-ax in the other.

Anakin raced from the opposite end of the plat-form, his lightsaber already activated. Krayn saw him and quickened his pace.

But Anakin was faster. With a leap, he landed in front of Krayn.

"It is time to pay for your crimes," he said.

"Not by the likes of you, boy," Krayn sneered.

Anakin attacked. He felt no fear. There was some-thing in his blood, something strange, as though ice now moved through his veins. It was not anger, he told himself. It did not feel like anger. It felt like justice. Purpose.

All the lives below in the factories, all the lives he had known on Tatooine, his mother, Hala, Amee, all who had suffered, they were in his hands. Everyone he'd lost, everyone he'd loved. Even Qui-Gon was here, urging him on, he felt sure.

He slashed out at Krayn. The pirate was quicker than he expected. Blaster fire singed the sleeve of Anakin's tunic. Anakin reversed and kicked out, hoping to dislodge the weapon from Krayn's meaty fist. But the pirate absorbed the blow and held on.

The *ping* of blaster fire followed Anakin as he somersaulted and landed to Krayn's left. The pirate dodged the first lightsaber pass and Anakin tossed the lightsaber to his other hand and came at him from a surprising angle. Krayn bellowed as the lightsaber grazed him.

He lifted the vibro-ax as though it were a toy, and came at Anakin from below. Startled, Anakin twisted away, but not before the vibro-ax grazed his wrist. The pain was blinding. If Krayn had been a centimeter or two closer, he would have severed his hand.

Anakin tossed the lightsaber back to his good hand. He leaped around Krayn and attacked from behind. Krayn turned and aimed the blaster. Anakin dodged the fire and moved forward, forcing Krayn to back up.

He felt righteousness pump through him. From now on, he would make no mistakes.

Memories pounded in him, of his mother, of Amee's tears for months after Hala was captured. He matched Krayn's viciousness with his own, driving him back toward the wall so he would have him at bay. He saw the first flicker of fear in Krayn's eyes and he enjoyed it.

"You will die at my hands, Krayn," he said through his teeth. "You will die at the hands of a boy."

Krayn was too exhausted to answer. His hair was wet and matted, and his powerful arm shook as he tried to raise the vibro-ax against Anakin.

Anakin had him now. He would show no mercy. Krayn deserved none. There was no capturing him. There was only killing him.

Obi-Wan had followed Siri from the conference room. As soon as they were alone, he whipped off his mask.

"I thought so," Siri said. "You were never good at disguise."

"I fooled you," Obi-Wan said. "Admit it."

She bared her teeth at him. "Never."

He followed her at a run to Krayn's quarters. He was not in his receiving room, or in the control center.

"He wouldn't go down to the factory," Siri said. "He wouldn't want to be anywhere near the rebellion."

They exchanged glances.

"The landing platform," Siri said, and took off.

They pounded through the corridors and burst out the exit. At the opposite end, Anakin held Krayn at bay. The pirate was bent over, breathing heavily. As they watched, a vibro-ax fell from his bleeding hand

and clattered to the ground. He lifted his face to his attacker.

"Anakin!" Obi-Wan shouted. He started toward him. Siri circled in case she needed to flank him for support.

His Padawan did not hear him. On his face was an intensity that Obi-Wan had never seen before.

Anakin raised his lightsaber to deliver the fatal blow.

"Don't!" Obi-Wan shouted.

The lightsaber slashed downward. Anakin sunk it in Krayn's chest. Krayn's mouth opened in a wordless scream. He locked eyes with Anakin. Then he toppled to the ground.

A few days later, Obi-Wan and Siri sat with Anakin and watched as the sleek silver transport set down on Krayn's landing platform.

"We'll certainly be returning to Coruscant in style," Siri observed. She looked more like her old self now, dressed in a simple tunic, her face scrubbed clean, her blond hair tucked behind her ears and gleaming in the weak sun.

"It's not often that a Senate delegation comes to congratulate us on a mission and give us a lift home," Obi-Wan said. "As a matter of fact, it's never."

"I guess they are grateful for the liberation of Nar Shaddaa," Siri said.

"Not to mention the downfall of Krayn and his pirate empire," Obi-Wan said. "The galaxy will be safer for many."

Anakin nodded. Obi-Wan studied his face. It was so

boyish and open. The glimpse he had seen of something dark, something feral, in the fight with Krayn was fading. The boy he knew had taken its place. Anakin had explained that Krayn still held a blaster. His life had been in danger. He had not violated the Jedi code by killing him.

Yet Obi-Wan still felt doubts. Doubts he could not share. Siri had not seen the expression on Anakin's face.

"Come, let's greet them," Obi-Wan said as the landing ramp came down.

"Wait, there's Mazie and Berri," Anakin said. "I have to say hello."

"Anakin, Chancellor Palpatine has come here himself," Obi-Wan reminded him.

Anakin grinned and ran his hand over his hair. "I know."

Obi-Wan nodded. Anakin was right. Because of Mazie and Berri, they had succeeded in their mission. The politicians could wait.

Mazie and Berri approached. Mazie was limping slightly. She had been wounded in the battle.

"We know you are leaving," Mazie said. "We could not let you leave without thanking you." She was speaking to all of them, but her gaze remained on Anakin. "You freed us all."

"You freed yourself," Anakin corrected. "It is I who should be thanking you." He turned to Berri. "And you, Berri. I'm glad to meet you at last. You showed great courage in helping Siri and me escape."

"I did only what I could," Berri said.

"That was a great deal," Siri said.

"The Colicoids have offered us wages to remain," Mazie said. "We will do so until we have enough to get off-planet. Nar Shaddaa is no place to live."

"Perhaps the Jedi can help with relocation and transport," Siri said. "We'll be in contact after we reach the Temple."

Mazie and Berri exchanged happy glances. "That would be very good," Mazie said. "Safe journey home."

Berri smiled. "You won't have to worry about pirates."

Mazie reached out and grasped Anakin's shoulders in a sudden display of emotion. "You have guaranteed our safety and our lives by killing Krayn. We will never forget it."

"I will never forget you," Anakin said.

The three Jedi turned and headed for the Senate delegation. Chancellor Palpatine smiled and held out his hands.

"The Jedi have brought freedom to Nar Shaddaa at last," he said. "Now we can begin to clean up this world. The Colicoids need our help, and we need theirs." He shrugged. "It is the price we pay for the liberation of Nar Shaddaa and the end of Krayn. The Senate thanks you for your great service to the galaxy."

The Jedi nodded respectfully.

"Now, come aboard. We have everything prepared for a comfortable journey back to Coruscant," Palpatine said. Putting a hand on Anakin's shoulder, he led the way to the ship.

Obi-Wan hesitated, Siri by his side. He watched as Palpatine bent his head close to Anakin's to speak to him. What was making him uneasy?

Was it the memory of what he'd seen on Anakin's face in the battle with Krayn? His Padawan had been in the heat of battle and afraid for his life. He felt that Krayn was about to shoot. He had every reason to kill him. He had not killed him out of anger and revenge.

Yet when Anakin had turned to face him fully, his expression had been so empty. His gaze held neither triumph nor distress. Only blankness.

He had been numb from the experience of battle, Obi-Wan told himself. He himself had felt the same at times.

I will not abandon him, Qui-Gon, Obi-Wan privately vowed. *I see what you see. I see how he struggles. I see his immense capacity for good.*

Siri moved closer to him. "It appears that your Padawan has impressed the Chancellor. He has great gifts."

"Yes," Obi-Wan agreed. "Yet he has so much to learn."

The vision of Qui-Gon in the cave of Ilum rose in his mind. He didn't know what the vision was trying to tell him, except to go on. He would go on. He would guide his gifted Padawan as best he knew how. He would not fail.